Elbridge Streeter Brooks

The true story of George Washington

Called the Father of his Country

Elbridge Streeter Brooks

The true story of George Washington
Called the Father of his Country

ISBN/EAN: 9783744747097

Printed in Europe, USA, Canada, Australia, Japan

Cover: Foto ©Raphael Reischuk / pixelio.de

More available books at **www.hansebooks.com**

"HE WOULD NOT TAKE AN UNFAIR ADVANTAGE." *See page 24.*

THE TRUE STORY OF

GEORGE WASHINGTON

CALLED THE FATHER OF HIS COUNTRY

BY

ELBRIDGE S. BROOKS

AUTHOR OF "THE STORY OF OUR WAR WITH SPAIN," "THE AMERICAN SOLDIER,"
"THE AMERICAN SAILOR," "THE TRUE STORY OF THE UNITED STATES,"
"THE TRUE STORY OF COLUMBUS," "LINCOLN," "GRANT,"
"FRANKLIN," "LAFAYETTE," AND MANY OTHERS.

ILLUSTRATED

BOSTON
LOTHROP, LEE & SHEPARD CO.

PREFACE.

As the second in the series of "Children's Lives of Great Men," following the life of Columbus, the discoverer, comes the true story of George Washington, the founder of the country which to-day calls him its father.

America has had no greater, no nobler, no truer man. Every land has honored him, every race has sung his praise. As the years go by, his real worth becomes more apparent and needs none of the over-wrought little stories that have so long been told to boys and girls, to strengthen his character or give point to his record. The true story of his life is fine enough and full enough to interest, to inspire and to help, without adding the things that would make a prig of the boy and a god of the man who was always a truth-teller, truth-liver, and truth-doer, both as boy and man.

One of the best of modern Americans, James Russell Lowell, who was born on the same day of the month as Washington, February twenty-second, wrote, shortly before his death, to a schoolgirl whose class proposed noticing his own birthday: "Whatever else you do on the twenty-second of February, recollect, first of all, that on that day a really great man was born, and do not fail to warm your hearts with the memory of his service, and to brace your minds with the contemplation of his character. The rest of us must wait uncovered till he be served."

Which is a good text for those boys and girls who may be led to read this true story of George Washington. The name of Washington is one which America will ever reverence, and one, before which, American boys and girls may well stand, hats off, "uncovered" in memory, respect and love.   E. S. B.

CONTENTS.

CONTENTS.

CHAPTER X.

CHAPTER XI.

CHAPTER XII.

CHAPTER XIII.

CHAPTER XIV.

LIST OF ILLUSTRATIONS.

LIST OF ILLUSTRATIONS.

LIST OF ILLUSTRATIONS.

THE TRUE STORY OF

GEORGE WASHINGTON

CALLED THE FATHER OF HIS COUNTRY.

· ———

CHAPTER I.

A BOY OF VIRGINIA, AND HOW HE GREW UP.

 I WISH to write for young Americans the story of their noblest man. His name was George Washington. One hundred and sixty years and more ago he was a helpless baby in a pleasant Virginia home. That home was a low-roofed, big-beamed, comfortable-looking old farmhouse on a hill that sloped down to the Potomac, the beautiful river that separates the present States of Virginia and Maryland. One hundred and sixty years ago there were no States in America. All the land, from Maine to Georgia, belonged to England. King George the Second was its owner and master, and the thirteen colonies into which it was divided were ruled by men

sent over from England by King George, and called royal governors.

The people who lived in these colonies were mostly Englishmen or the sons and daughters of Englishmen, except a few thousand Dutchmen in the colony of New York, who had been conquered by the English many years before, and were gradually becoming English in manners and speech.

The old farmhouse of which I speak overlooked the Potomac River, and the plantation to which it belonged was called Bridge's Creek, because, there, a little stream of that name flowed into the Potomac. All about it was farm-land or forest. There were then but few

A DUTCHMAN.

cities in America. New York and Boston and Philadelphia were the largest and almost the only real cities, and they were small enough when compared with the cities of to-day. The colony of Virginia, however, was the richest and most populous of all the thirteen English colonies along the Atlantic. Its people were farmers; the richer ones owned great farms or plantations upon which they raised tobacco for the English market. The plantation of Augustine Washington at Bridge's Creek on the Potomac, was one of the large ones; it was in Westmoreland County, on the Virginia side of the Potomac, and not many miles from where the river empties into the Chesapeake Bay; the Washington plantation contained a thousand acres, and stretched along the Potomac for fully a mile. The old house in which Augustine Washington and his wife Mary lived was built years before by his grandfather, the first of the Washingtons who came to America. It is said that the Washingtons came originally from a thatch-roofed sandstone house in the

THE SANDSTONE COTTAGE AT LITTLE BRINGTON.
(Said to have been the English home of Washington's grandfather.)

English village of Little Brington; but this is not clearly proved. It is enough to know that Grandfather John Washington came to Virginia in 1657 and built the house on Bridge's Creek. It was not a mansion. It was a plain, old-style Southern farmhouse, with steep, sloping roof and

projecting eaves, with a broad piazza in front, a great chim
ney at either end, and just such a big, delightful attic as boys
and girls love to play in, on days when the wind blows and
whistles without, or the rain pours and patters on the roof.

It was to this old Virginia farm-house that Augustine
Washington, in the year 1730, brought home his second wife,
Mary Ball, of Lancaster County, Virginia; but whom, so it is
said, he met and married in England.   In the old house
were two boys of seven and nine years; they were Lawrence
and Augustine; their mother, their father's first wife, had
been dead nearly two years, but their new mother became almost like an own mother to them.

In this old farmhouse at Bridge's Creek, the eldest son of
Augustine and Mary Washington was born on the twenty-
second of February, 1732.   They named him George.
What with his two half-brothers, Lawrence and Augustine,
and his own brothers and sisters who were born after him,
George Washington had plenty of company in his home.
He never remembered the house in which he was born, however; for in 1735 some sparks from a bonfire set it in flames
and it was burned to the ground.

Not a stick nor a stone of that old house remains to-day;
but it has been a famous spot for many a year.   In 1815,
a memorial stone was placed on the spot where the house
once stood, and on the stone were these words:

*Here, on the eleventh of February, 1732, George Wash-
ington was born.*

What is called the "old style" of reckoning time was used in those days, and the eleventh of February was in 1732, the same as the twenty-second of February to us; therefore, under our modern way of reckoning time the birthday of George Washington was the twenty-second of February — the day that we celebrate as a National holiday.

When his house at Bridge's Creek was thus destroyed, Augustine Washington moved into another farmhouse that belonged to him on another plantation, further up the Potomac. This plantation was in Stafford County, and did not border on the Potomac River, but was on the banks of the Rappahannock, nearly opposite the little town of Fredericksburg.

This house was very much like the one that was burned. It stood back from the river, on a ridge or bluff that overlooked the

MONUMENT ON THE SITE OF WASHINGTON'S BIRTHPLACE.
(*By permission of John Crawford & Son, Designers.*)

Rappahannock, and between the house and the river was a stretch of meadow that was the playground of the Washington children. For in this pleasant old Virginia country home George Washington lived until he was sixteen years old. As with the birthplace of Washington, so it was with the home of his boyhood. It was long since destroyed, and nothing marks the spot where, as a boy, he who was to be the " Father of his Country " lived and played and dreamed and thought and grew. It would be pleasant to know more about his boyhood days, for it is always interesting to know what sort of a " bringing up " a great man had when a boy. But there is, really, very little known about the boyhood of George Washington.

His father was what we should call a " well-to-do " farmer. He owned several large

CHILDREN OF WASHINGTON'S TIME.

farms, or plantations, as they were then called, in the colony of Virginia, along the Potomac River. He never had much money, for money was not plentiful in those "old colony days." Planters and farmers were rich in land and in the crops they raised, but these crops were not always sold for money; they were exchanged for the things that were needed on the farm or in the home. The Virginia farmers,

as I have told you, raised more tobacco than anything
else; for a great many folks in Europe had learned to
smoke tobacco since the time when Sir Walter Raleigh (who
introduced into England the practice of smoking tobacco) was
drenched from head to foot by his terrified servant who, seeing the tobacco smoke, thought his master was on fire. So
the rich Virginia farmlands were planted with tobacco, and
the ships that came from England took away the tobacco,

WASHINGTON'S BOYHOOD HOME.

and left in exchange things to eat and things to wear, and
things to make home comfortable.

And a very comfortable home the son of this Virginia
planter had. It was not a great nor a grand house, as were
a few of the houses of the very richest Virginians; it was
not, perhaps, what the boys and girls of to-day, with to-day's
idea of comfort, would call comfortable. It was a story and
a half house, with a low sloping roof, with great chimneys
and fireplaces at either end, and with half a dozen "roomy"
rooms, one of which had its fireplace bordered with the

funny Dutch tiles and was called the "best room." There
were no carpets on the floors, no gas, nor oil, nor coal, nor
stoves for light and heat; the furniture was neither elabo-
rate nor plenty; the books were but few, and the household
games and toys made for girls and boys to-day were then

unknown. No bicycles, no postage stamp
albums, no tennis nor croquet, nor baseball
— what could the "sons of gentlemen" find
to do when Washington was a boy?

Well — they had plenty to eat and drink;
there were horses to ride and guns to shoot
with and dogs to hunt with; there were fish
to be caught and out-of-door games to be
played, and the boys were just as full of fun
and just as ready to play as they are to-day.

The Washingtons, as I have told you,
were considered "well off," although they had
not much money to spend and did not live in
a grand house; so the sons of the smaller

A GOOD DEAL OF A
BOY.

planters, the boy who belonged to what was known as the
"poor white families," and the little black and white servant-
boys — for there were both kinds in Virginia then — looked
upon George Washington as a good deal of a boy, and followed him as their leader in their out-of-door sports and
games.

When he was a little fellow, eight or nine years old, he
had a pony named Hero, that "Uncle Ben," one of his

father's slaves, taught him to ride; and he owned a "whip-top," something rare in those days. And this he considered so fine a possession that he wrote about it to his friend Dickey Lee (afterwards a famous American), and generously told him, "You may see it and whip it." But, best of all, he liked the free life out of doors, the rough-and-ready boy play that gives health and strength and vigor and muscle to boys, and fits them to become robust and active men.

When he was eleven years old, in April, 1743, his father died suddenly, and Mary Washington had the management of the great plantation and the houseful of children. How well she succeeded we all know; for, to-day, George Washington's mother is almost as famous as her son. One of the older boys — George's half-brother Lawrence — had been sent to England to school; but, when his father died, there was scarcely money enough to do this for the other boys; so George got what small schooling he obtained in the simple country schools about his home, where he learned little more than what was called " the three R's "— reading, 'riting and 'rithmetic.

So he grew up at home a brave, generous, quiet, manly boy. He loved to roam the fields and row and swim in the rivers, and talk with the other boys as to what he should like to do or be when he grew up. For the Virginia boy of one hundred and fifty years ago, there were great attractions — dangers are always attractive — the sea and the forest. George Washington, going down to the tobacco sheds on

the wharf which was a part of every plantation, would talk
with the men who had sailed across the sea from England,
and listen to their hair-breadth escapes from wreck and
pirates (for there were fierce pirates sailing the seas in those
days) and he would think he would like to be a sailor; then

IN THE TOBACCO SHED.

at other times he would talk with the hunters who came in
with the "peltry," about the great forests that stretched
away, no one knew how far to the westward, and that were
believed by the boys to be full of all kinds of dangers and
all sorts of ferocious monsters, and then he would think he
would like to be a hunter.

But after all I imagine he was ready, just then, to agree that it was not a bad thing to be a boy on a big Virginia plantation with plenty of servants and horses and dogs and boy comrades, and with a watchful mother whom, if he had to obey strictly, he loved dearly.

He was strong, he was active, he was healthy, he was

GOING TO THE "FIELD SCHOOL."

happy — big for his years, strong, for a boy, the best wrestler ("rassler," they all called it then), the best runner, the best rider among all the boys of his section. He grew to be what are called in these days an athlete. Not a boy could "stump him" successfully or unsuccessfully, or "dare him" to any feat of boyish strength or skill. He studied faithfully — he always did everything thoroughly — but he did

not really enjoy his schools. What he did enjoy when he
went to the little log school-house (called a " field school ")
near his home, was his corn-stalk brigade. For William
Bustle and some of the schoolboys played they were French

while George Washington and other of the
schoolboys played they were Americans,
and with cornstalks for guns and gourds for
drums, the rival soldiers played at charge and
skirmish and furious battle, and the Americans, led by Captain Washington, were
always victorious.

With such a father and mother George
Washington could not have been other than
a good boy. And he was. He was big and
strong, and sometimes mischievous and careless — fearing nothing and daring much, as
such big, good-natured, quiet and determined
boys are apt to; but he hated a lie; he was
never mean, nor low ; he never did an under-

PREPARING FOR A
"BASSLE."

hand action; and he knew that the first lesson a boy needs to
learn is obedience to parents, respect toward older people,
and kindness to all.

Some folks will tell you that Washington had no boyhood; that is to say, he was not one of those fun-loving, fun-
making boys we all like to know. But I wish you to believe
otherwise. I wish you to feel that George Washington,
as a boy, though quiet and thoughtful, was just as fond of

fun and of sport, just as careless, reckless, and boisterous, just as high-strung and as boyish a boy as are any of you who read his story, and who, in the schools and homes of America to-day are, because of this Virginia boy of long ago, learning, hoping and meaning to be loyal, true and helpful American men and women when you grow up.

CHAPTER II.

WHY THE BOY WHO WISHED TO BE A SAILOR BECAME A SURVEYOR.

EVERYBODY likes a boy who is strong and manly, and that was what George Washington was. The boy who, while in his early teens, could tame an unbroken colt, firmly keeping his seat until he had mastered the wild and plunging thoroughbred, the boy who could "down" the best wrestlers in the county, who could throw a stone clear across the Rappahannock, toss bars and pitch quoits better than any man or boy about him, and sight and fire a rifle held with one hand only ; the boy who could always be trusted to keep his promises, tell the truth, and do as he was bid without asking why, was a boy who could be at once bold and brave, good and gentle, sturdy and strong, wise and cautious.

If he tamed the unbroken colt, killing it rather than let it master him, he did not excuse himself nor lie about it to his mother when the trial of will was past. And, if he mastered the thoroughbred, (as he once did in a wager of his head against the horse) he would not take an unfair advantage, nor accept the horse as his because he had neither kept his seat nor fully kept his claim of ability.

MARY THE MOTHER OF GEORGE WASHINGTON.

He would get dreadfully "mad" with other boys sometimes, and he was so strong that if he had been at all bad, he might have been what is called a bully. But, even when he was a small boy, he had learned to control his temper; and this he always did throughout his useful life, losing it so seldom and only when there was every excuse for his getting "mad," that we can set this splendid habit of self-control as one of the things that made him great and noble.

But as he got into his teens and began to think for himself, he felt that he must soon decide upon what he was to do for himself so as to take some of the burden from his mother's shoulders. Mary Washington had a great

"HE TAMED THE UNBROKEN COLT, KILLING IT RATHER THEN LET IT MASTER HIM."

plantation to look after and not enough money to do the things she wished. She saw this big, spirited, ambitious, determined son of hers growing up in her home, and she wondered what she could do for him and with him, to make him a capable and successful man, who, by helping himself, should help her.

The boy thought of the same thing, too. He really could

"HE EVEN TRIED ON A 'SAILOR SUIT' AND POSED BEFORE HIS FRIENDS."

not tell what he wanted to do, for not many boys of fourteen are ready to know what they are best fitted for. From being much along the river, however, when the busy tobacco ships sailed into the harbors and along from wharf to

wharf, or slipped down with the current to the broad bay
and the wide ocean beyond[George Washington soon grew
to have that desire for travel and adventure that comes to
many a brave boy, and so he concluded that he should like
to be a sailor, even if he had to go "before the mast," on
one of the tobacco ships. / He talked with his older brothers
and with his big-boy friends about it. He even tried on a
"sailor suit" and posed before his friends. They all thought
it might be a good thing for him, and said that some day he
might rise to be a mate or perhaps a captain. ('There is lots
of risk about going to sea, they said. Vessels get wrecked
and pirates sometimes capture them, and there is a chance
that the bold sailor boy may be drowned or have to walk the
plank. But then, too, there is plenty of promise in a sailor's
life for so plucky a young fellow as George Washington,
and even if he does start in as a sailor on a tobacco ship, he
may some day get a berth in a man-of-war and wear the
king's uniform in the king's navy.

All this only made George Washington the more anxious to go to sea. He talked it over with his mother and,
although she greatly disliked the idea of her son being a
sailor, still she was so impressed with the boy's desire to do
something, and to be somebody, and to go somewhere "on
his own hook," that she was just on the point of saying yes
to his pleadings when something happened to make her
say no.)

This was the receipt of a letter from her brother in

REAL ESTATE DEALERS OF THE OLDEN TIMES.

England, to whom she had written about her son George and his desire to ship as a sailor on one of the tobacco-carrying vessels that sailed between the Potomac wharves and English ports. "Do not let him go to sea," the letter said. "Make a tinker or a tailor of him, or anything that will keep him on shore, rather than see him sail away from you as a

LONGING FOR HOME.

sailor before the mast. A sailor on one of these trading vessels is worse off than one of your negro slaves. He has not a moment he can call his own; he is kicked and cuffed and robbed and beaten; not a dog but has an easier life. If he hopes to get into the king's navy, the chances are small for he knows no one who could get him a berth, and there are hundreds of boys waiting to get in who have a better chance than he. And suppose he should stick to his trading life and get to be captain of a tobacco ship — why, any small planter in Virginia is better off than one of these shipmasters. Tell the boy not to be in too great a hurry to get rich. Tell him to take things easily, to be patient and careful, and he will be much better off in the end than if he should go to sea."

This letter settled the question. Mrs. Washington decided against the sea-fever, and though she knew her son was a manly and adventurous boy, she felt that there were

just as good chances for him to get a footing and make his
way on shore as on sea.

So the lad gave up his dream of the free life on blue
water that had so long filled his thoughts. It was enough
for him that his mother said no, even though he wished so
much for her yes. He never thought of acting contrary to
her decision or counsel; and when he grew to be a man and

DREAMING OF GOING TO SEA.

was making a name
for himself, Mary
Washington's opin-
ion of her son was
more to him than
all the big words of
the world. "George
has been a good boy," she said, "and I am sure he will do
his duty."

Back to school went the boy who had longed to be a
sailor. Near his birthplace at Bridge's Creek, where his
half-brother Augustine had built himself a house, there was
a fairly good school kept by a Mr. Williams; and to him the
boy was sent.

George Washington was always good at figures. He
was correct and careful over them, and promised to became
what is called a good mathematician. Mr. Williams taught
him surveying. That, you know, is the science of measur-
ing land so that the owner can know just how much he
owns, just how it lies, and just where its boundary lines run.

For when he knows that, he can cut it up into tracts or lots of given sizes, and set all the measurements down on paper in lines and figures.

This is a very important work, especially in a new country, where people own large tracts of land, and other people, coming there to live, wish to buy new tracts or purchase parts of old ones. It requires a clear head, a good eye, and quickness and correctness at figures. All these, George Washington had. He was fourteen years old when he gave up going to sea and went to study mathematics and surveying under Mr. Williams. When he was nearly sixteen, in the autumn of 1747, he left school and went to visit his half-brother, Lawrence Washington, at his new home on the Potomac, which he called Mount Vernon.

THE BOY GEORGE'S HANDWRITING AT 13.

Lawrence Washington was nearly twelve years older than his half-brother George, but he loved the boy and was always trying to help him along. Lawrence, as I told you, was sent to school in England; he had gone to the wars with the squadron of the gallant admiral Vernon, and had fought under that brave leader at Porto Bello and Carthagena, where the Spaniards were whipped, but where so many brave American soldiers and sailors died of fever and pestilence. After the wars were over, Lawrence Washington came back

to Virginia, married Miss Fairfax, and settling on the Potomac plantation his father had left him, built a house and
called his place Mount Vernon, naming it for the gallant admiral with whom he had gone to the West Indies to fight
the Spaniards.

Near to Mount Vernon was a plantation of the Fairfaxes

RIDING OFF TO BELVOIR.

called Belvoir. George
Washington used to ride
over to Belvoir to see
George Fairfax, who was
a few years older than
himself, and there he met
a man who had much to
do with starting him out
in life. This was a queer
and odd old English
nobleman, Thomas, the
sixth Lord Fairfax. He
was a descendant of that
great Lord Fairfax who
had fought with Crom-
well against the first King
Charles, and helped the second King Charles to get his
crown again. This Lord Fairfax whom George Washington
knew had, at one time, lived in the highest society in England. He was a scholar, a writer, a soldier and a fine
gentleman; he was very rich and very high and mighty

"LAND SURVEYING HAS ITS RISKS."

at home, but, because the girl he was to marry suddenly decided to marry some one else, Lord Fairfax "got mad" (as great Lords and small boys will some times, you know). He left England forever and sailed across the sea to America, where he owned acres upon acres of land among the Virginia mountains. This great tract of country had been given by King Charles the second to Lord Fairfax's grandfather. And when this Lord Fairfax found out what a fine country Virginia was, and how rich the land was, he determined to live there and improve his property.

People had been going upon his lands without leave and settling upon it — "squatters," they were called — and Lord Fairfax found that he needed some one who was bright and bold and strong, who could go all over his great possessions (which included nearly one-fifth of the present State of Virginia), determine their boundaries, mark down the pieces that the squatters had taken possession of, and get everything ready toward what we call, to-day, "developing" the property.

Lord Fairfax met George Washington at

Beginning the Eleventh Day of November 1749

Washington

WASHINGTON'S HANDWRITING AT 17.

Belvoir and Mount Vernon. He talked with the young man, rode with him, hunted with him, took a fancy to him, and, discovering that he was a correct and reliable land-surveyor, asked him to "take the job" of going all over the Fairfax possessions in the beautiful Shenandoah Valley and among the Virginia Mountains. "Locate the land," he said, "survey it, settle its boundaries, note down the roads and highways and report to me about the people who have settled themselves on my land without leave, and who must be either driven off, or satisfactorily arranged with. And you may have plenty of adventures, too. Land surveying has quite as many risks as a sailor's life."

It was a splendid opportunity for the sixteen-year-old boy. It was just the start in life he needed, for it was just what he understood, just what he could do, and just what he liked. It would make a man of him. And it did.

So, at sixteen, he became a land-surveyor. He was a handsome young fellow, almost six feet tall, well-shaped though a little lean, long-armed, strong and muscular. He had light-brown hair, grayish-blue eyes, a firm mouth, a frank and manly face and he had a way about him that made people like him, though he was so quiet and retiring, while there was a look on his face that made them obey him if he was in a position to counsel or direct.

Even as a boy, you see, George Washington had what we call the qualities of mind and brain, the courage, the caution and the determination to succeed that made him, in after years, a leader of men and the chieftain of America.

CHAPTER III.

HOW THE SURVEYOR BECAME A SOLDIER.

 IS there any boy who does not enjoy life out-of-doors, especially if he is strong, healthy, active, adventurous and observing?

George Washington and George Fairfax started out on their surveying expedition in high spirits, ready to face the hard work and the rough life they knew lay before them, prepared to take things as they came and make the best of everything. That is the only way for any boy to "tackle" a piece of work successfully; for fretting makes work all the harder and brings no enjoyment out of life. And George Washington never fretted.

The boys were out among the hills with the compass and the chain for five weeks, during the months of March and April, 1748. That is the time of year when Virginia streams are swollen and Virginia mud is plenty. The young fellows were often hungry, often wet, often cold and uncomfortable; they slept in flapping tents and smoky cabins; they faced dangers and risks and hardships; but none of these things worried them. They met with trappers and tramps and Indians; they worked and hunted and fished; they climbed mountains, forded rivers and made their way along roads that were "execrable" and trails that were uncertain. But they were healthy, hearty, manly boys and they had "such a good time" that, when they returned to the settlements, George Washington was quite ready to try it gain.

"THEY FACED DANGERS AND RISKS AND HARDSHIPS."

He did his work as a surveyor so well and brought back such excellent results of his five weeks' trip that Lord Fairfax felt that the boy-surveyor had been a credit to him. He not only gave the lad more work of the same sort, but he so influenced the royal governor of Virginia, who had the "say" in all such matters, that young George Washington was appointed as one of the "public surveyors" of the colony.

This gave him plenty to do. For the next three years he was kept busy laying out tracts of land in the Shenandoah Valley and along the Potomac. Whenever a person buys a piece of land they either have it surveyed again or they accept the figures of the last survey as correct; and so good a surveyor did George Washington make, so correct were his measurements and so reliable his figures that, to this day, his surveys have stood unquestioned; and, long after his death, the lawyers whose duty it was to look up such matters, when land was passed from one owner to another, declared that the only old-time surveys in Virginia that could be depended upon as correct were those of George Washington. A pretty good record for a boy-surveyor, is it not?

And in all this hard, out-of-door life and work, Washington was laying the foundation for that future of health and strength, of decision and determination that helped him so much when he grew to be a man and had the affairs of an army and a nation to look after. His rough life in the forest and on the hills made him watchful and cautious; his mixing with all sorts of people made him study the ways of men and taught him how to act toward them; the keen air and the bright sunshine were better than medicine; he grew stronger and sturdier, his frame filled out and his muscles hardened, so that when he was nineteen, after three

years' experience as a surveyor, he was one of the manliest
and one of the stoutest and one of the handsomest young
men in the whole colony of Virginia.

And now came a new experience. For the first and only
time in his life, George Washington left his native land.
His older brother, Lawrence Washington, to whom he was

"BETTER THAN MEDICINE."

indebted for help and counsel and
kindness, had never really recovered
from the fever that had attacked
him when he was fighting the
Spaniards at Carthagena. In 1751
his health broke down completely
and he had to seek a warmer cli-
mate. So he went to Barbadoes,
in the West Indies, and he had
George go with him as helper and
companion. But for a time he was
obliged to do without his brother's
help, for George, who had never
been vaccinated, caught the small-pox in Barbadoes and was
very sick. His strong constitution helped him through,
however, and when he was well again he sailed back to Virginia to bring Lawrence's wife to join her sick husband
at Barbadoes. But before he could return the invalid himself
came home to die.

Lawrence Washington's death was a great blow to his
brother George. For young George loved Lawrence dearly

and was joined with him in numerous plans and enterprises, such as are always undertaken in a new country. Chief among these was a great land speculation known as the Ohio Company.

The Ohio Company was an association of rich men in England and in Virginia who bought great tracts of land beyond the Virginia mountains. They offered fine opportunities to people who would make their homes on these lands. For this would render the land so valuable that the owners would be able to get a great deal of money for the tracts left for sale after the new country had been thus "opened up" for settlement. The lands of the Ohio company were mostly in West-

YOUNG WASHINGTON AT BARBADOES.

ern Pennsylvania. This region, it was claimed, was within the boundary of Virginia, as was also the vast stretch of western country which is now occupied by the great States of Ohio, Indiana, Illinois, Michigan and Wisconsin.

But England was not the only nation that held possessions in North America. Canada belonged to France, and the French also had land in the South, so that they claimed all the Western part of America on a line running from Montreal to New Orleans. To enable them to hold and occupy this country, the Frenchmen had built a chain of sixty forts. If you look on the map and pick out the cities of Montreal, Ogdensburg, Detroit, Toledo, Fort Wayne, Vincennes, Natchez and New Orleans, which have grown up where once certain of these French forts stood, you can see what a vast tract of country France said she owned and was ready to defend, in North America.

FRANCE IN POSSESSION.

So when the Ohio Company began to send out surveyors and road-builders into their lands in the West, the Frenchmen grew excited and said that the Englishmen were trying to steal their land. They prepared to defend what they claimed to own, and made ready to build a new chain of forts, from a spot where the city of Erie now stands on Lake Erie, southward to the Ohio River.

Now Lawrence Washington had been the American

manager of the Ohio Company. When, therefore, the French-men began to grow warlike and Virginia talked of fighting back, Lawrence had secured from the royal governor of the colony of Virginia, whose name was Dinwiddie, an appoint-ment for his brother George, then a boy of nineteen. This position gave George Washington charge of the militia-men who might be called upon, in the country about Mount Vernon, to fight against the French.

After Lawrence Washington's death in 1752, and while George, who had charge of his affairs, was looking after matters at the saddened home at Mount Vernon, Dinwiddie, the royal governor of Virginia, was getting ready to deal with the Frenchmen who were becoming more and more troublesome in the Ohio country. It was necessary to do something at once to stop their insolence, for they were annoying the English settlers and stirring up the Indians who had been friendly to the English. Indeed, unless some-thing was done at once, the Frenchmen would own the whole western land.

"We must send some one into the Ohio Country to see and talk with these Frenchmen," Governor Dinwiddie said; "we must find out what they mean by coming into our king's dominion, building forts on English land, interfering with our settlers and stirring up the friendly Indians. Whom shall we send?"

And Lord Fairfax, the wise but odd old nobleman who had been George Washington's friend, said to the Governor:

" I know just the man.   You need a messenger who is young
and strong and brave; one who knows the country; who is
clear-headed, can deal with the Indians, and will not be afraid
to tell the Frenchmen just what is right.   Send George
Washington."

So George Washington was appointed Commissioner to
the French Posts in the Ohio Company.   He was provided

Through the Wilderness.

with the paper that
showed to all people
that he was Com-
missioner.   Then,
supplied with letters
to the French Com-
mander,   Major
George   Washing-
ton,   as   he   was
called, aged twenty-
two, set out from
Williamsburg, the
capital of the colony
of Virginia, on the
thirtieth of October,
1753.   He was to undertake a perilous journey of over a
thousand miles; he was to ask the Frenchmen what they
meant by their fort-building and their loud talk, and to tell
them, in the name of the King of England and the Governor
of Virginia, to leave the Ohio Country at once.

He went to say good-by to his mother, who was living in the old house at Fredericksburg on the Rappahannock. Then he engaged an old Dutch soldier named Van Braam, from whom he had learned how to fence, to go with him and talk French to the Frenchmen (for Washington could not speak French); he hired, also, a good guide named Christopher Gist, and a man named Davidson who could talk with the Indians in their own language; besides these, he took four frontiersmen, who knew all about traveling and camping in the forests, and could take care of the tents, the horses and the supplies. And, when all was ready, he set out from Will's Creek on the Potomac (now Cumberland in Western Maryland), on the fifteenth of November and at once pushed straight into the wilderness.

It was a hard and dangerous journey. Over the mountains and through the wilderness, across rivers and along narrow trails the young Commissioner and his men traveled westward, winning back some of the leading Indian chiefs who had gone over to the French, until, on the twelfth of December, he stood before the French commander, the Chevalier de St. Pierre, and delivered his letters.

Of course the Frenchmen refused to leave the land they claimed as their own. The French commander was very polite and pleasant to the young Virginia commissioner; but that was all. He gave Washington a letter to Governor Dinwiddie, and after staying in the French fort a few days, Washington and his men turned their faces toward home.

It was on Christmas Day that they started to return, and it was anything but a merry Christmas. The weather was very cold, the roads were terrible, the rivers were swollen and full of floating ice, the Indians were treacherous and

WASHINGTON AND THE FRENCH COMMANDER.

unfriendly. Anxious to get back as quickly as possible, Washington set out on foot, dressed like an Indian, and accompanied only by Christopher Gist, leaving the other men and the horses to come on as well as they could.

The two men had a journey filled with peril and adventure; but when at last, on the sixteenth of January, he reached Williamsburg, alone, and delivered to Governor Dinwiddie the answer of the French commandant, all men praised him for his courage, his persistence, his firmness, his self-possession, and said: "Well done, George Washington!"

No one had expected that he would get rid of the Frenchmen. He had not been sent with that purpose. He had simply gone as the messenger of the king to bid them begone and to bring back their reply.

Orders were at once issued to build a fort upon a point reported on by Washington as the best spot in the Ohio country from which the English could defend their rights. This spot is where the important city of Pittsburg now stands. Men were sent out to build it, and

WASHINGTON IN INDIAN DRESS.

soldiers were to be raised at once in Virginia to hold the fort against the French.

The fort was built, the soldiers were enlisted and Major George Washington was appointed to drill them and get them ready to march against the French in the spring. He had hard work; but, by spring, two companies of soldiers were ready. Joshua Fry was made colonel of the Virginia forces; George Washington was appointed lieutenant-colonel and dispatched to the Ohio country. With one hundred and fifty men, on the second day of April, 1754, he set his face westward again, and, going over the road he had travelled the year before, marched westward toward the French.

It was a poor enough showing with which to face the warlike and soldierly Frenchmen, who might object to the building of the English fort. But it was the best he could do, and he hoped when he was safely within the new fort to be a match for any force the Frenchmen might march against him. But alas! when he came near the place, he heard strange and most unpleasant news. The men who had been sent to build the fort had been driven away by a large force of Frenchmen who had surprised them at their work. The half-finished fort had been pulled down and a new one built in its place by the Frenchmen, who were now marching eastward to meet Washington and his Virginians, and capture them or drive them away.

Thus, you see, France struck the first blow. For to take a fort from another nation in time of peace, is what is called "an act of war." Washington was greatly disturbed at the news, for he had only a part of the soldiers who were to be sent forward and the Frenchmen were a thousand strong. But he was not the man to turn back. He sent a messenger to Governor Dinwiddie and to the governors of

GEORGE WASHINGTON AND CHRISTOPHER GIST.

Pennsylvania and Maryland asking for more soldiers; then he marched on to a spot he had in view where he hoped to be able to build a good enough fort to hold the Frenchmen at bay until help came to him.

At a place called Great Meadows he came upon a French force led by Ensign Jumonville, and a sharp fight took place. Jumonville was killed, some of the Frenchmen were taken prisoners and the war had really begun. [It was a war that was not to end for seven years; it was to drive France out of America and was to set France and

AT GREAT MEADOWS.

England fighting each other, in Europe as well as America. It was to train Americans for the great conflict for liberty which they were to wage against the king and parliament of England, and to bring to renown this young Virginian surveyor who fired the first shot of the war in this little battle at Great Meadows, and who on that day, the twenty-eighth of May, 1754, became a soldier and a conqueror.]

CHAPTER IV.

COLONEL WASHINGTON OF MOUNT VERNON.

THE brave man — like the boy who is really brave — does not rush blindly into danger; but, if he is brought face to face with it, he acts boldly and quickly. This was Washington's way. He had been victorious in the little fight which he had been forced to make, but he knew that, if more fighting were to follow, as he felt sure it would, he must stand his ground firmly and try to hold his own.

"I will not be surprised," he wrote to the Governor of Virginia, begging for the soldiers that had been promised him; "and you may hear that I am beaten. But you will hear at the same time that we have done our duty, in fighting as long as there was a shadow of hope." These were brave words for a young leader in the strait in which he found himself, but it was George Washington's way of doing things all through his life.

A few more soldiers were sent to him and with these troops and his Indian helpers he marched on to meet the French. With the new men came the news that Colonel Fry who was to lead them on, was dead. Washington was therefore in chief command of his little army. He was Colonel Washington now.

After he had marched through the mountains, he heard that the Frenchmen, a thousand strong, were moving towards him. He was in no safe place to give them battle, so he fell back to Great Meadows and finished a hastily-made fort of logs and dirt, which he well named Fort Necessity. Here on the third of July, 1754, the French found him.

At once the dauntless courage of Washington asserted itself. If they wish a battle, let them have it now, he said; and, throwing open the door of his flimsy little fort, he marched with his men out into the open meadow, daring the Frenchmen to a fight.

But they did not accept his "double dare." Instead, they staid in the woods and fired at the Americans, not showing themselves where they could be fought openly. So Washington marched back into the fort again, and for nine hours the Frenchmen battered and besieged it.

Then they sent word to Washington that it was of no use for him to hope to whip them, as they had four times as many men as he had and everything was in their favor. " Give us up the fort," they said; " return the prisoners you have taken; promise not to build any more forts around here for a year, and we'll call it square and let you go home without any more fighting."

Washington hated to agree to this; but when he came to look things over and see how useless it was for him to try to beat the French, with his men half-starved, his powder gone and his Indian helpers running away, he remembered the old proverb that says, "the better part of valor is discretion." So he agreed to the French terms and, on the fourth of July, gave up his crazy little fort and marched back toward home. He had been defeated,

BITS OF OLD WILLIAMSBURG.

but he was by no means conquered.

Still, he felt very badly over the way things had turned out. If the help that had been promised him had only been given, he would perhaps have told quite another story. But when he got back to Williamsburg he found that people looked upon him as a hero and praised his brave and gallant attempt; he was publicly thanked for what he had done and told to fill up his regiment and march once more against the French.

But he knew that such a plan was foolish. "We must not try to fight the French until we are all ready," he said. "When enough men have been raised to make such an expedition wise, you can depend upon me; but there is no sense in marching to certain defeat. And that is what an attempt now would mean."

So the Virginians set about raising a thousand men; but when the English officer who was to have charge of the troops said that Washington, not being a regular soldier in the British army, but only an American militiaman, could not be a colonel but only a captain, Washington refused to accept such a command. It was no way, he declared, to treat a man who had been asked to lead; and rather than be so used, he said, he would give up his commission. And he did, retiring to Mount Vernon, which had been given to him by Lawrence Washington when he died.

The next year things were different. The King of England and his advisers determined to make a stand in America against the French. So they sent over two regiments of British troops, under command of a brave soldier whose name was Major General Braddock, and told him to get what help he could in Virginia and drive out the French at once.

General Braddock came to Virginia with his splendid-looking fighting men. When he had studied the situation there, one of the first things he did was to ask Colonel George Washington of Mount Vernon to come with him as one of his chief assistants, called an aid-de-camp.

Washington at once accepted. He saw that, now, the King of England "meant business," and that, if General Braddock were as wise as he was brave, the trouble in the Ohio country might be speedily ended and the French driven out.

But when he had joined General Braddock he discovered

that that brave but obstinate leader thought that battles were to be fought in America just the same as in Europe, and that soldiers could be marched against such forest-fighters as the French and Indians as if they were going on a parade. This made Washington feel very badly and he did all he could to advise caution.

BRADDOCK.

It was no use however. General Braddock said he was a soldier and knew how to fight, and he didn't wish for any advice from these Americans who had never seen a real battle.

At last everything was ready, and in July, 1755, the army, led by General Braddock, marched off to attack the fort which the French had built at Pittsburg and had named Fort Duquesne.

Washington had worked so hard to get things ready that he was sick in bed with fever when the soldiers started; but, without waiting to get well, he hurried after them and caught up with them on the ninth of July, at a ford on the Monongahela, fifteen miles from Fort Duquesne.

The British troops, in full uniform, and in regular order

as if they were to drill before the king, marched straight on in splendid array. Washington thought it the most beautiful show he had ever seen; but he said to the general: " Do not let the soldiers march into the woods like that. The Frenchmen and the Indians may even now be hiding behind the trees ready to shoot us down. Let me send some men ahead to see where they are and let some of our Virginians who are used to fighting in the forest go before to clear them away." But General Braddock told him to mind his own business, and marched on as gallantly as ever.

BRADDOCK'S HEADQUARTERS IN WEST VIRGINIA.
(*From a recent sketch*)

Suddenly, just as they reached a narrow part of the road, where the woods were all about them, the Frenchmen and Indians who were waiting for them, behind the great trees and underbrush, opened fire upon the British troops, and there came just such a dreadful time as Washington had feared. But, even now, Braddock would not give in. His soldiers must fight as they had been drilled to fight in Europe, and, when the Virginians who were with him tried to fight as they had been accustomed to, he called them cowards and ordered them to form in line.

It was all over very soon. The British soldiers, fired upon from all sides and scarcely able to see where their ene-mies were, became frightened, huddled together and made all the better marks for the bullets of the French and Indians hiding among the trees and bushes. Then, General Braddock fell from his horse, mortally wounded; his splen-didly-drilled red-coats broke into panic, turned and run away, and only the coolness of Washington and the

ON THE MARCH.

Virginian forest-fighters who were with him, saved the entire army from being cut to pieces.

Washington fought like a hero. Two horses that he rode were killed while he kept in the saddle; his coat was shot through and through, and it seemed as if he would be killed any moment. But he kept on fighting, caring nothing for danger. He tried to turn back the fleeing British troops; he tried to bring back the cannons, and, when the gun-ners ran away, he leaped from his horse and aimed and fired the cannons himself. Then with his Virginians, that Brad-

THE INDIAN ALLIES OF THE FRENCH RETURNING HOME AFTER BRADDOCK'S DEFEAT DRESSED IN THE SPOIL OF
THE BRITISH ARMY.

dock had so despised as soldiers, he protected the rear of the
retreating army, carried off the dying general and, cool and
collected in the midst of all the terrible things that were
happening, saved the British army from slaughter, buried
poor General Braddock in the Virginia woods and finally
brought back to the settlements what was left of that splendid army of the king. He was the only man, in all that
time of disaster, who came out of the fight with glory and
renown.

After that, you may be sure his advice was followed.
When another army was raised, and, after three years of waiting and preparation, the soldiers, at last, were ready to go
once more against the French, Washington's plans were
adopted; his way of doing things was followed out, and he
was appointed Commander-in-Chief of all the forces in
Virginia.

He did not seek the command; he did not want it. But
it was Washington's way never to say no to what seemed to
be his duty. "If it is in my power to avoid going to the Ohio
again," he wrote to his mother, "I shall. But if the command is pressed upon me by the voice of the country, it
would be dishonorable in me to refuse it." That is the
way that office should be accepted and duty looked at by
every man and by every boy, and, as I have told you once
before, that was Washington's way.

Once more British soldiers were sent to Virginia, and
with them, marching westward, went Washington and his

Virginians. But the English government had learned wis
dom through defeat, and things were better done this time.
Soldiers were sent to fight the French in Canada, too, and
the gallant Frenchmen found their hands so full that they
had to give up some of the things they hoped to keep. So
when the British and Virginians, in the Ohio country, came
to the fort they had been so long trying to capture, the
French had gone away, and Washington and his men marched
into the ruined and smouldering fort, where, not many years
after, the town of Pittsburg was built.

Then he went home again. He was now the leading
man in Virginia and, though only twenty-six, he was famous
throughout all the Colonies as a brave and daring leader, a
wise and safe adviser, a cautious and clear-headed man.

MRS. MARTHA WASHINGTON OF
MOUNT VERNON.

Soon after his return to Mount
Vernon he married a wife. This was
Mrs. Martha Custis of White House.
She was a wealthy, charming, brown-
eyed widow of twenty-six. To her Washington had become engaged, just before
his last march against the French.
They were married on the sixth of
January. 1759. and if any boy or girl wishes to know what
a fitting wife to a great man this Virginian woman proved,
let them read. when they are older, Washington Irving's long
life of George Washington and his wife, Martha.

Three months after his marriage, Colonel Washington

took his seat in the Virginia legislature, then called "The House of Burgesses." He had been elected a member while with the troops at Fort Duquesne, and when he took his seat, the speaker, or presiding officer of the House of Burgesses, publicly thanked him for his honorable record in the war.

Washington was surprised, but feeling that he ought to

THE OLD CAPITOL AT WILLIAMSBURG IN VIRGINIA.
(Where the House of Burgesses met.)

say something, he rose to reply. He was never a ready or what is called "extemporaneous" speaker; so he hesitated, and blushed and did not know what to say; whereupon the speaker said: "Sit down, Mr. Washington. Your modesty equals your valor, and that surpasses the power of any lan-

guage I possess;" which was a very pretty and very just
compliment, was it not?

Washington and his wife, and the two little children of
Mrs. Custis, Martha and John Parke Custis, began life at
Mount Vernon. The property had grown very valuable.
Mrs. Washington was wealthy, and the farmer's son of the
Rappahannock plantation was now Colonel Washington of
Mount Vernon, and one of the richest men in Virginia.

Mount Vernon was a real Virginia mansion. It was a
large, two-story house with four rooms on each floor; a high
and broad piazza ran along the front and looked down upon
the beautiful Potomac, flowing past the estate. Across the
river were the fields and forests of Maryland, and all about
the house stretched the broad acres of the Mount Vernon
plantation. Here with his dearly-loved wife and her children, with a large estate to look after and care for, with
health and wealth and friends and the respect of his neigh-
bors and fellow-citizens, George Washington settled down,
as he thought, to the life of a country gentleman, of which
he wrote, " I hope to find more happiness in retirement than
I ever experienced in the wide and bustling world."

And, for a time, he did find much happiness there. He
loved the busy life indoors and out. He was fond of riding
and hunting, and we hear of his splendid horses — Magnolia,
the Arabian, and Blueskin, his favorite iron-gray, and his
hunting-horses, Chinkling, and Valiant and Ajax; we hear
of his dogs Vulcan and Ringwood and Music, Sweetlips and

WASHINGTON'S SEAL AND COAT OF ARMS.

COLONEL GEORGE WASHINGTON
OF MOUNT VERNON

AND

MRS. MARTHA CUSTIS
OF WHITE HOUSE,

*Married at St. Paul's Church, near
White House, Virginia, on the
Seventeenth of January, 1759.*

COLONEL AND MRS. GEORGE WASHINGTON OF MOUNT VERNON.

Singer and Truelove, Forrester and Rockwood and the rest; we read of his riding "after the hounds," as it was called, to hunt the black fox or the gray, and how, with his huntsman, "Billy Lee," he took the field at sunrise, dressed in a short blue hunting jacket, a scarlet waistcoat, buckskin breeches, top-boots, velvet cap and carrying his long-thonged whip.

Mount Vernon welcomed many visitors, for one of the chief rules of a Virginia home in those days was : Welcome ! and How d'ye do ! to all. This open hospitality was always part of Washington's nature, and even in his early days, the young colonel and his wife had a host of friends. In fact, to be without company was so rare an event, that Washington would write down the fact in his diary, and he said that, though he owned more than a hundred cows, he had to buy butter.

He was as strong and healthy as ever. When he was forty years old he could throw the heavy hammer farther than anyone else; no man could ride better, none could walk further, none was of a more noble and commanding presence than Colonel George Washington. He kept note of everything that was going on in the colonies and in England; he was a leader in politics and church work, in generous and helpful deeds, and in all that makes a man a good citizen, a kind neighbor and a faithful friend.

So he grew on from young manhood to middle age, and, for over fifteen years, lived as a well-to-do country gentleman at Mount Vernon.

Then came the events that made America free and made Washington famous; but, before that glorious end was reached, there were many dark and bitter days, and many a time that tried the courage, the temper and faith of this great and noble man.

CHAPTER V.

HOW JOHN ADAMS OF MASSACHUSETTS SAVED THE COUNTRY.

WHEN a boy or girl has tried to do a hard sum in arithmetic and has succeeded, something is obtained besides the answer: it is confidence. The French and Indian war was the hard sum set for the American colonies, and, when it was over, when Canada was conquered and the French soldiers were driven out of America, the thirteen colonies cried out: "We helped to do it; we got the answer to the sum ourselves!" They begun to see how strong they were, if they joined together to do anything, and when England attempted to make them pay out money without the right to say for what that money should be spent, the colonies said: "See here! that is not fair. The money is ours; you have no right to take it from us nor to use it without our having anything to say about it."

But England was just like General Braddock. She was obstinate and determined to have her own way, and she said to the colonies, as Braddock did to Washington : "You mind your own business! You haven't anything to say in this matter, but must just do as I tell you to."

There were now two millions of people in the thirteen colonies ; they were no longer separate sections, caring nothing about any colony except their own : they had sent men to the army who side by side had fought the French and Indians. Thus the people of Massachusetts and of Virginia, the men of New York and of South Carolina, had been brought to know each other better and to believe that the one way for the colonies to be prosperous and successful was to be united and friendly, to form a partnership to govern themselves, and to be, not English colonists, but Americans.

So when the British government tried to force money from them by unjust taxes, the colonies objected ; then they " talked back " ; then they resisted, and dared the King of England to " come and get it." For twelve years the quarrel went on. England said America should or — ; America said she wouldn't, unless — ; then she dropped the " unless " and said she wouldn't anyhow, and, when the British government attempted to back up its threats, the men of the colonies stood up with guns in their hands ; there was a sharp fight between the American Minute Men and Lord Percy's red-coats on Lexington Common and another by the old North

Bridge at Concord, and the war of the Revolution had begun.

Like a great many other thoughtful men in America, George Washington had feared trouble from the first. He saw that England would never consent to allow her American colonies to have anything to say in this matter of taxing and spending; he knew that America was growing so strong and united that she would not long be willing to be England's "good little girl," to do as she was told and ask

THE FIRST MARTYRS FOR LIBERTY.

no questions, and he knew that it meant more than simply talking back to one another; he knew that it meant, if neither side would give in, a war between the colonies and the king; and "if that comes to pass," he said, "more blood will be shed than history has ever yet furnished instances of in the annals of North America."

In September, 1774, the thirteen colonies sent their best men to Philadelphia to meet and talk things over in the building known as Carpenters' Hall. This convention is now known as the First Continental Congress. George Washington was one of the men sent by Virginia, and although he did not make any speeches — he was always a silent man, you know — he worked quietly and left the talking to others. The wisdom of his advice and the way in which he tried to bring all the members of the Congress into friendship and harmony were so noticeable that, when one of the members was asked whom he considered the greatest man in the Congress, he answered at once: " If you mean the man who knows the most and has the best judgment, Colonel Washington of Virginia is unquestionably the greatest man on that floor."

The First Continental Congress told King George some plain truths. " You must not treat your American colonies so meanly," they said. " We will not stand it. If we can have nothing to say in your parliament, then we will not do as you say. If we are to be taxed, then we must say how the money we pay shall be spent."

But such talk only made King George and his ministers angry and they went on the same as before. So when Washington returned to his home at Mount Vernon, he told the people: "We must get ready to do something." The man who had said: " If necessary, I will raise a thousand men, subsist them at my own expense and march to the relief of Boston," was now ready to make good his word. He began to drill soldiers, and wrote to his brother that, if need be, he would accept the command of the soldiers from Virginia and that it was his full intention to devote his life and fortune to the cause.

In May, 1775, the second Continental Congress met at Philadelphia. Its members had heard the news from Lexington and Concord, and now had come together for serious business. The royal governors had run away as soon as the trouble began; the colonies had to look after themselves and they said they could do this much better without the royal governors. So they told the Congress to govern the united colonies and to make laws for that purpose.

Congress also took charge of the soldiers that hurried to Boston after the bloodshed at Lexington and Concord, ready to fight the red-coated soldiers of the king. But these soldiers must have a leader. Whom should he be?

There were, in this Congress, certain men who wished to "go slow" and try to "patch things up" with King George and his ministers. There were others who felt that they were great men and ought to be in the highest position. There were still others who were not yet Americans, but thought only about the good that could come to his own colony. It is so with all new movements, about which there is any uncertainty, but all these men, in time, came to be patriotic and splendid Americans.

So, when the question arose as to who should be the commander-in-chief of the American army at Boston, there was at first some hesitation. The soldiers facing the British there were mostly New England "minute men" and

militia men, and some of the members of Congress thought
a New England general should be their leader. The Southern members wanted an American army made up from all
the colonies, with a general appointed from the South. For
several days nothing was done. Time was precious. The

THE FLAG ON BUNKER HILL.
(" *Come over if you dare,*" *it said to the British in Boston.*)

army must be gathered at once if a bold stand was to be
taken ; and if Congress was to take charge of the soldiers at
Boston, Congress must give its army a leader.

Then John Adams of Massachusetts stood up in Congress. He was an active and able man, who saw that some-

thing must be done at once, and, having looked the ground over knew there was but one man in America to be selected for this high command. "I have but one gentleman in my mind," he said, addressing the Congress. "He is a certain gentleman from Virginia who is among us and is well known to us all. He is a gentleman of skill and experience as an officer; his independent fortune, great talents and excellent universal character would command the approbation of all the colonies better than any other person in the Union." Everyone knew whom John Adams meant; everybody looked in the same direction, and a modest gentleman, dressed in a colonel's uniform of blue and buff, hurriedly rose and slipped out of the room. But John Adams's words decided the question. The result of the debate was that, on the fifteenth of June, 1775, his proposition was accepted and George Washington of Virginia was unanimously elected commander-in-chief of the Continental Army. Thereupon the new leader, now General Washington, rose in his place to thank the Congress for the honor conferred upon him ; and, to his words of acceptance, he added these: "I beg it to be remembered by every gentleman in the room that I this day declare with the utmost sincerity I do not think myself equal to the command I am honored with." Then, adding to his modesty a patriotic generosity, he refused to accept any of the salary set apart for his services and promised an exact account of all his expenses.

It was a great honor, but it was a great responsibility.

As such Washington looked upon it when he accepted the command. "It is a trust too great for my capacity," he wrote to his wife; "but it has been a kind of destiny that has thrown me upon it, and it was utterly out of my power to refuse it."

Did you ever make a promise that you felt was what the boys call "a big contract?" But, if you were a plucky boy or a conscientious girl, you tried hard to carry out your promise, did you not? It was just so with Washington. He had said, "I will command your army." And yet none knew better than did he, how little the fighting men of the colonies were like the trained troops of England that they must face in battle. They were patriotic, brave and determined; this he knew, but they were untrained, undisciplined and unprepared for war; there was but little money to meet the expenses of a struggle with a great and wealthy nation; they had no one to help them, no friends to lend them money and every man felt that he had something to say about how things should be done.

So he rode on toward Boston. And as he rode, escorted by a troop of horsemen, tidings came of the Battle of Bunker Hill. There had been a fight, people said, in which the British had stormed the fortifications of the Americans and finally driven them out. It looked like a defeat.

"Why did they retreat?" General Washington asked the hard-riding messenger whom he met on the road to New York, galloping to Congress with the news.

"DID THEY STAND THE FIRE?" WASHINGTON ASKED ANXIOUSLY.

"For want of ammunition," the messenger replied.

"And did they stand the fire of the British regulars as long as they had ammunition?" Washington asked anxiously.

"That they did," the post-rider cried enthusiastically, "and held their own fire in reserve until the enemy were within eight rods."

A look of relief and satisfaction came to Washington's face. "Then the liberties of the country are safe, gentlemen," he said to Generals Schuyler and Lee who accompanied him. And he rode forward, feeling that a defeat which proved the pluck and fighting qualities of the Continentals was really no defeat but a victory.

"THAT THEY DID," THE POST-RIDER CRIED.

UNDER THE ELM ON CAMBRIDGE COMMON GEORGE WASHINGTON TOOK COMMAND OF THE AMERICAN ARMY.

If Washington had imagined that his fame was known only to Virginia the greetings that he met on his long ride from Philadelphia to Boston opened his eyes to quite the opposite. He was the commander-in-chief; upon him all the hopes of the people rested; and, as he rode from town to town, men and women, boys and girls came out to meet and welcome him and bid him God speed. At New Haven the boys from Yale College met him with a band of music, and who do you suppose led the band? Why, a boy named Noah Webster, who afterwards made the two books that we use in our schools to-day — Webster's spelling-book and Webster's dictionary.

So he rode on to his duty, the foremost man in America. And, on the morning of

THE OLD ELM AT CAMBRIDGE.

Monday, the third day of July, 1775, General George Washington rode into the broad pastures known as Cambridge common, and, beneath the spreading branches of an elm tree, which still stands — an old tree now, carefully preserved and famous through all the land — he drew his sword and in presence of the assembled army and a crowd of curious and enthusiastic people, he took command of the Continental Army as General.

He was forty-three years old — just as old as Julius Cæsar when he took command of the army in Gaul and made himself great. Just as old as Napoleon when he made the great mistake of his life and declared war against Russia. But how different from these two conquerors was George Washington. What they did for love of power he did for love of liberty — sacrificing comfort, ease, the pleasures of home and the quiet life he loved, because he felt it to be his duty.

As he sat his horse, like the gallant soldier he was, under the Cambridge elm that warm July morning, he was what we call an imposing figure. He was tall, stalwart and erect, with thick brown hair drawn back into a queue, as all gentlemen then wore it, with a rosy face and a clear, bright eye — a strong, a healthy, a splendid-looking man in his uniform of blue and buff, an epaulet on each shoulder, and, in his three-cornered hat, the cockade of liberty. And the commander-in-chief of the Continental Army looked upon the army of which he had assumed command and determined to make soldiers of them and lead them on to final victory.

MEDAL PRESENTED BY CONGRESS TO WASHINGTON AFTER THE EVACUATION OF BOSTON BY THE BRITISH.

CHAPTER VI.

HOW GEORGE WASHINGTON LOST AND WON.

ALTHOUGH General Washington may have felt what is called a pardonable pride as he sat upon his horse, under the spreading branches of the Cambridge elm, and drew his sword as " General and Commander-in-Chief of the Forces of the Thirteen United Colonies," he knew that he had no easy task before him. But he went to work at once, as he always did when he had anything to do, and tried to make real soldiers of the farmers and fishermen and store keepers and working-men who made up the Continental Army. So well did he work, and so closely did he keep the British

Army shut up in Boston, that King George's red-coats were obliged to leave the city — evacuate it, is the military word — and, in March, 1776, Washington was in possession of the town in which the British had declared they would crush the rebellion and conquer the rebels.

This was Washington's first success, and it showed the world that the Americans " meant business," that they were not to be easily overcome by the trained soldiers and generals of King George, and that the Commander of the Continental Army was a born leader of men, and knew how to go to work to win.

But none knew better than did that Commander how

THE BRITISH EVACUATING BOSTON.

hard the winning would be. His troops had yet to meet the British soldiers in the open field and, after the evacuation of Boston, England began to find out that if America was to be whipped into obedience, there must be plenty of men sent over to do the whipping. But England could not spare enough of her own soldiers, and so she tried to hire fighters from other nations. She tried to hire twenty thousand Russian soldiers, but failed; then she tried to get some from Holland, and failed. But, at last, she hired from certain states of Germany called the Hesses, first eighteen thousand men, and then more and more, until, before the Revolution was over, nearly thirty thousand of these hired soldiers, or mercenary troops, called "Hessians," were brought over the sea to fight, in the armies of England, the freemen of America. Many Englishmen were indignant at this hiring of foreign soldiers to shoot down their relations in America, and you may be sure it did not increase America's love for England.

A HESSIAN.

The first lot of Hessians sailed into New York harbor in August, 1776, and joined the army of Sir William Howe, who thus had a force of nearly thirty thousand men to face Washington's poor little army of scarcely ten thousand men. The battle that had to follow took place at Brooklyn on Long Island, on the twenty-seventh of August, 1776. It was, of course, a total defeat for the Americans. It could not be otherwise. And when Lord Howe, the British general, had

defeated the Americans, killed a great many, taken a great
many prisoners, and driven the rest within their entrench-
ments at Brooklyn, he said: "To-morrow evening will bring
the fleet up the river and, with an army on one side of the

THE COMING OF THE HESSIANS.

rebels and our ships on the other, we will 'bag' the whole
army and crush the rebellion."

But the trouble with Lord Howe, as with the other British generals, was that he did not understand Washington.
The American leader expected to be defeated. He knew
that his troops must be drilled into an army before they

could successfully face the soldiers of King George, and it was this patient courage that George Washington showed, in the midst of defeat and danger, all through the Revolution, that was one of the things that made him great.] So, while he gathered his defeated army within the lines at Brooklyn, he saw through Lord Howe's plan to capture him, and without waiting for the too-confident British general to try his plan, he determined to save his army by a retreat to New York. It was a dangerous experiment. If the British knew that he was trying to escape them, they would swarm down upon his little army and capture or destroy it. So he went to work carefully. He got together all the boats he could, marched his men about, as if he meant to get them ready for a battle the next day, and then, silently and swiftly, got them down to the river. Here the boats, with the fishermen soldiers of a Marblehead regiment at the oars, were rowed over and over again ; the fog shut them out from view, and before morning the soldiers were all ferried over, Washington crossing in the last boat. He had saved his army and showed the thing that makes a great general -- knowing how to retreat as well as how to fight. For a successful retreat is sometimes quite as much a victory as is a successful battle.

It was much the same with what follows. By this time America had spoken. The thirteen colonies, through their representatives in Congress, had declared that they would no longer acknowledge King George as their ruler, nor En-

gland as their governing power, but that they were. " and of
right ought to be, free and independent states." This was
done in a paper called the Declaration of Independence,
drawn up in Independence Hall in Philadelphia, when Congress was in session, and issued on the fourth of July, 1776,

THE LAST BOAT.
(*Washington at the retreat from* **Brooklyn.**)

a little over a month before the disastrous battle of Brooklyn.
I think most American boys and girls are dissatisfied
because George Washington did not sign the Declaration
of Independence. He was the greatest American; that was
America's greatest deed. Why should he not have signed it?

Of course, you know that he was with the army. His duty was there and not in the Con-

INDEPENDENCE HALL, PHILADEL-
PHIA.
(Where the Congress met.)

ROOM IN WHICH THE CONGRESS MET.

HALLWAY.

gress; for when of the Continen- his seat in Con- knows just how bringing Con- that resulted in dependence. He he became the general tal army he gave up gress. But no one much he did toward gress to the action the Declaration of In- wrote and talked and argued to show the men in Congress that the colonies could not longer remain subject to England. They must be independent, he said. And though George Washington's name is not signed to the famous Declaration, he had as much to do with it as had many men who really did sign it.

But when the Declaration of Independence had been signed, it meant that it must be backed up by deeds. So, though the battle of Brooklyn was a defeat followed by a retreat, and though the world said that the colonies could never secure their independence, Washington never weakened, but kept on struggling and striving, though defeats and retreats followed one another until any but the most determined leader would have been discouraged and felt like giving in.

Washington retreated from Brooklyn to New York, and when the British followed him there, he retreated across the Harlem into Westchester County. Still pressed by Howe, he retreated across the Hudson into New Jersey, and finally across the Delaware into Pennsylvania, with Howe still following him up. It was almost like a game of checkers, was it not?

His army now consisted of but three thousand men. His soldiers were ragged, his equipment poor, his situation desperate. The winter was a hard one, and so nearly lost seemed the cause of the colonies, that new soldiers could not be induced to serve in the army ; all this time, too, the enemies of Washington — for there were leading men in Congress and out of it who said all kinds of hard things about him, and tried to have him set aside in favor of some general whom, they declared, was more of a fighter — were active against him.

And still Washington kept silent. He was biding his time. In New York, Lord Howe said that the end was near at hand, and that the rebels would give up the fight before New Year's Day, if he did not capture them before that time.

And then, when no one expected it, Washington acted. He had determined upon a bold move. This was nothing more nor less than an attack upon the Hessian lines at Trenton.

He made all his preparations secretly, cautiously and carefully. He was to cross the Delaware from the Pennsylvania side and, if possible, take the Hessians by surprise. Other soldiers were to march to his assistance from Philadelphia and from Bristol, and cut off all hope of escape. And the river was to be crossed on Christmas night.

It was anything but a merry Christmas when, with twenty-five hundred picked men, Washington came to the banks of the Delaware and tried to set his small army across. The river was filled with great cakes of floating ice; it was so cold that two of the soldiers were frozen to death, and, before morning came, the air was filled with icy and cutting sleet. It seemed the very worst time to attempt such an enterprise as Washington had determined upon. So bitter was the night, indeed, that the other generals who had been ordered to march to his support gave it up, because they did not see how they could cross the icy Delaware.

But Washington crossed the Delaware. And at eight o'clock the next morning his ragged, half-frozen soldiers attacked the village of Trenton, in which the Hessians were stationed. He drove in their pickets, surrounded their camp,

WASHINGTON CROSSING THE DELAWARE.

fought them through the town, killed their commanding officer, and captured nearly all of them, though some five hundred or so managed to get away.

Then with his thousand prisoners, Washington re-crossed the Delaware, and the long spell of failure was broken. The brilliant deed he had done paralyzed the over-confident British, put new life into the suffering cause of liberty and so inspired the colonies that, where men had been unwilling

to risk their lives for a failing cause, they were now ready to
join one which seemed to promise success. Washington
had saved the Revolution. From the fight at Trenton dated
the steady march toward victory.

That sharp and successful fight, too, showed how great a
general was Washing-
ton. The retreat from
Brooklyn had been one
proof of this; but that
was a retreat. The cap-
ture of the Hessians at
Trenton showed him to
be a leader who could at-
tempt the most daring
move, and, once at-
tempted, could push it
through to the end,
though everything
seemed against him.

The great German
soldier-king whom his-
tory calls Frederick the
Great, when he heard

GEORGE WASHINGTON.

*(Painted by James Peale, when Washington was Commander-in-
Chief of the Army. Now in Independence Hall.)*

how, with a few ragged regiments (so footsore, indeed, that
their march could be tracked in the snow by the blood from
their unprotected feet), Washington had defeated and captured the European soldiers whose business was fighting

and whose equipment was perfect, declared that Washington was a born soldier and that the attack at Trenton was the most brilliant campaign of the century.

Washington knew when to strike, and then he struck. In the darkest hour of the Revolution he took the chance of defeat and death, and by a movement that gave his name strength and showed the world his ability, he secured a victory which, because of its daring, its brilliancy and its completeness, set the world to thinking and created friends and helpers for the struggling thirteen colonies along the Atlantic coast of North America.

CHAPTER VII.

HOW ONE MAN DID IT ALL.

YOU may be sure that when the British found that Washington had been too smart for them and, just when they thought him weakest, had made the sudden and successful dash on the Hessian camp at Trenton, they rubbed their eyes in a bewildered sort of way and set their red-coats charging after him. But just when they thought him hemmed in between them and the Delaware river, all of a sudden he disappeared. In the morning the British found the burning camp-fires of the Americans, but no Americans. Washington had slipped away in the night by cross-roads and by-paths; and, before the British knew what he was about, he had fallen upon what was called their "reserves"—three fine regiments at Princeton—and had driven them away with considerable loss.

You see what a perplexing sort of a foeman this George Washington was. The British never knew just how to take him. When they expected him to fight, he didn't; when they expected him to run away, he didn't; and, when they thought they had him safe and fast, that was just the time he would slip from their grasp or fall upon them at some unexpected point and, as the saying is,

WASHINGTON AT PRINCETON.

"whip them out of their boots." It was all wrong; it wasn't at all the thing they expected. But it was war, and it proved, what England finally found out, that George Washington was a great general.

IN CAMP. — WASHINGTON LISTENING TO THE BOY FIFER.

As a great general is a great leader, and as the leader, whether in statesmanship or in sport, in business or in school, as boy or as man, is the one whom all finally look to when anything is to be done that requires judgment, courage, coolness and decision, so George Washington, growing stronger and greater as time went on and the things he had to decide upon or to do, tried and developed him, became the one man in America to whom all America looked for suggestion, guidance and decision. In other words, he was the one man who did it all.

He planned the campaigns that gradually led to victory; he insisted on having an army, instead of Continental militiamen who only joined to serve as soldiers for what is called a brief term of enlistment; he borrowed money himself or got rich men to lend it to the feeble colonies, to pay the expenses of their army; he saw ahead the plans of the British, felt certain they would try to weaken him by sending armies to attack the colonies at the North and South, and he so planned things that the enemy was whipped, and Burgoyne and his army captured at Saratoga in New York, and would have been beaten back at Charleston in South Carolina if the general in command had but done as Washington told him. He tried to have Congress do something more than talk and run away from the British; he held the people together by his firmness and his courage when things seemed all going the wrong way; he kept the army from breaking up altogether when Congress would not send the soldiers

money to pay for their work or to save them from starving.
It was his advice that brought about the "alliance" with
France, as it was called ; it was his letters to Congress that
kept that body from doing many unwise things, and things
that would have spoiled all that he had undertaken or had
done.

All this would have turned the heads of smaller men, as
it turned the head of Napoleon and made him a usurper when

AT VALLEY FORGE.

he should have
been a patriot. But
George Washing-
ton was great in
every way, and
thought nothing of
personal benefit or
what he could make
out of anything for
himself. And yet
he had his enemies.
All through the
dark days of the
war, when things
seemed to go so slowly, when the British still held the cities
of Philadelphia and New York, when the American army
was shivering in Valley Forge or changing their camps in
New York and New Jersey, there were ambitious men in
Congress, and jealous men in the army who tried to push

Washington from his position of command, saying that he was slow and did not know how to do things, and that they or their favorite generals, if they could but have the chance, would end the war in a short time.

But Washington cared no more for them and their doings than if they had been flies buzzing about him. His purpose was to defeat the British and establish in the land the liberty that had been declared for America on that famous fourth of July in 1776. Nothing could turn him from his purpose; he had the people behind him; they honored, trusted and loved him and, with enough men in Congress to back him up and try to give him what he must have — men, money and guns — he set his face toward success, and worked steadily ahead.

Through danger and defeat, through suffering and loss, through jealousy and treason and discouragements on every side, Washington kept on — retreating, advancing, fighting. He proved to the world, by the battle of Germantown, that his raw fighters were becoming real soldiers. He showed that he knew when not to fight, as at White Marsh, and how to turn a rout into a victory as at Monmouth. He kept a lost cause alive in the log huts of the winter quarters at Valley Forge; he bothered the British and kept them so uncertain as to just what he meant to do, that they could not send troops to help their soldiers who had marched into the northern and southern country; and thus he made the battle of Saratoga, and the storming of Stony Point, and the fight

at Bennington, and the engagements at the Cowpens and
and Guilford Court House and Eutaw Springs, in none of
which Washington took part, victories that hastened the
end.

The end came at Yorktown in Virginia on the nineteenth
of October, 1781. What that end was, and how it came
about, every boy and girl
in America who reads or
studies the history of the
land knows. Through the
efforts of Benjamin Franklin, another great American,
the French king who hated
the English because En-
gland had taken Canada
from France, sent over men
and ships to help the Americans, and declared that, so
far as France was concerned,
it recognized the rebellious
colonists of America as a

A DASH AT MONMOUTH.

new nation in the world. Sixteen war-vessels and four
thousand men came across the water; but, as Washington
feared, their help did not amount to so much, except that
it frightened the British and made them think that all
Europe was going to join to help free their American
" rebels," as they kept calling the revolted colonies — what

boy or girl knows the difference between a revolution and a rebellion?

France did help the United States very much, however, in the way of lending money and supplies for carrying on the war; and, surely no one in America, now or ever, will

CARVING THE HAM. — HOW MONEY WAS SMUGGLED THROUGH THE BRITISH LINES TO THE CAMP AT VALLEY FORGE.

forget the name of that gallant young French nobleman, the Marquis de La Fayette, who, when scarcely more than a boy, hired a vessel and ran away to America to help fight for its freedom, becoming a dear friend to Washington, a ready helper, a cautious leader and a daring soldier of liberty.

But in the summer of 1780, the French help began to amount to something.   Rochambeau with six thousand

BARTHOLDI'S STATUE OF LAFAYETTE.
(In Madison Square, New York.)

Frenchmen landed at Newport in Rhode Island, and joined Washington and his soldiers at Peekskill in New York.   In 1781, the Count de Grasse sailed into Chesapeake Bay with more ships and soldiers; Washington and Rochambeau hurried to Virginia and, almost before the British knew what was happening, Lord Cornwallis and a British army of nine thousand men were penned up in Yorktown in Virginia.

The British general was brave and able; he tried to get away, but could not; Washington set his soldiers to digging earthworks, and soon had the British camp surrounded, and after three weeks of firing and fighting, the British general gave in, and on the nineteenth of October, 1781, he surrendered to General Washington.

This ended the Revolution.   The king of England could

SURRENDER OF CORNWALLIS AT YORKTOWN.

not get men to serve in America; the people and parliament
were tired of war; the Americans were really taking care of
themselves and had done so for five years; they were determined not to give in; France and other nations had helped, or
were ready to help them, and so, on the thirtieth of November,
1782, Great Britain acknowledged the in-
dependence of the United States; on the
third of September, 1783, the paper that
did this, and was called a treaty of peace
between Great Britain and the United
States of America, was signed at Versail-
les in France, and on the twenty-fifth of
November, 1783, the last red-coated soldiers of the king left
the country they had failed to conquer, and America was
free.

One of the French Soldiers.

And who do you think could have felt more thankful or
more joyful over the way things had turned out than George
Washington? Although many things had not gone as he
desired, still the end he had worked for had come about, and
America was free. He thanked the French who had helped
him, he wrote to Congress congratulating the country on
the success that had come at the ending of seven years of
war, and set about trying to so finish things up as to avoid
the troubles that he felt must come if everything was not
done "decently and in order." To get the very thing we
want is sometimes the worst thing for us, and the results of
victory have often been the most serious problem for men to

face. For it is hard to be modest and patient and obliging
when we have, at last, obtained what we have worked and
fought for. America's most serious problem was now to come,
and none knew this better than did George Washington —
the man whose hand and head had made his country free.

CHAPTER VIII.

WHY THE GENERAL LOST HIS TEMPER.

 I HAVE said that although the war ended with
the surrender of Cornwallis at Yorktown,
none knew better than did Washington, that
the trouble was by no means over. He understood, indeed, what many could not see,
that one struggle could only lead to another,
and that peace with England did not mean
peace in America, so long as things remained
unsettled and uncertain.

You remember, of course, the fable of the frogs who overthrew King Log only to get in his place King Stork, a
much worse tyrant. America had achieved independence;
she was a free nation; but you must remember she was made
up of thirteen states, which, as colonies, were selfish, and

which, as states, were also selfish. To be sure, the common danger of war, and a common dislike of England, had bound them together, so that they were not so entirely wrapt up in their own affairs or so jealous of one another as they had been when they were simply English colonies, but they were all of them, as we say, "looking out for number one;" they were governing themselves as separate states, without regard to Congress and, in fact, all that Congress could do was just to carry on the war and look after the matters that the war created for all the states.

This looking out for "number one" made the states careless as to the matters which they thought belonged to Congress to attend to, while it made Congress careless and "touchy," according as they were left alone or interfered with by the several state governments.

In no way was this carelessness more unfortunately shown than in the treatment of the soldiers. They were the men who had struggled and suffered and starved that America might be free. You would think that Congress would look after them with especial care, and see that they had good food and warm clothes, and money to send home to their wives and children. But Congress did not, and almost one half of Washington's time seems to have been spent in writing to Congress, pleading the cause of the neglected soldiers whom, from raw and undisciplined recruits, he had drilled and made into victorious fighters.

Well, Yorktown came, and the war was over. Congress

and the people threw up their hats and hurrahed and shouted Victory! and Hallelujah! But that did not pay the soldiers.

Of course you may ask, why, how could Congress pay the soldiers if it had no money and no power to make the states pay up. That is true, but it

"MAD ANTHONY" WAYNE.
(One of Washington's bravest Generals.)

should have so worked as to compel the states to pay their shares of money due the soldiers, or borrowed enough from foreign nations or wealthy men to keep its promises to Washington and his men. But it did not, and the soldiers grew more and more angry, and begun at last to say that if Congress had not power enough nor strength enough to keep its promises to the soldiers who had fought its battles, then Congress was "no good," and the best thing for America was to have a government in which one man should have the "say," and see to it that what the soldiers had done they should be paid for.

Now, here was just where one of the things that made up the greatness of Washington was shown. He knew just how the soldiers felt; he could not blame them for being angry; he, himself, was angry over the delay and indifference of Congress and the state governments. The soldiers loved him; they looked up to him, and were always ready to obey him, going where he sent them and doing what he told them.

The army was a power in the land.   Had it wished, it could
have said to Congress: "Get out; go home! we have conquered England; we have freed America; we will put some
one in to 'run' this country better than you can do," and
Congress could not have stopped them.   All they needed
was a leader.   Had George Washington been the kind of
man of whom you may read in Roman history, of whom the
soldiers made emperors and the people first obeyed and then
murdered, he need only have said to the soldiers: "You are
right.   I will lead you, and we will soon settle things;" and
he could have been, as was Cæsar, as was Cromwell, as was
Napoleon, under almost the same circumstances, first, leader,
then dictator, then king.

But George Washington was not that kind of a man.
He was truly great.   As a result of all this murmuring and
fault-finding and grumbling and threatening, the soldiers did
try to do something desperate.   Through one of their general's trusted officers, they sent him a letter saying just what
I have told you they thought — that Congress was a failure;
that the army had whipped England and won independence
for America; that England's government was, after all, more
strong and safe than could be this jumble of thirteen separate states; that some such government, like that of England,
would be best for America; that such a government needed
a head, who might be called a protector, dictator or king;
that there was only one man in America worthy to fill such a
position; and they hinted (though the letter did not say this

in so many words, it meant it all the same) would General
Washington take control of the government of America by
the help of the army, and be crowned king of America?

Then, for once in his life, George Washington was angry.
There had been other times when he let his "angry passions
rise," but they were not numerous. Washington was naturally a quick-tempered man, one who, if he did not watch over
himself, would "get mad" easy. But, in his early days, he
had learned the first step toward greatness; he had learned
to conquer himself, and no man ever tried harder and succeeded better than he to live up to the old saying we read in
the Bible: "He that is slow to anger is better than the
mighty; and he that ruleth his spirit, than he that taketh a
city." But he would get angry sometimes, and there were
two things he could never stand — treachery and cowardice.
He was always enraged if men turned and ran in battle.
That was what made him swear at General Lee at Monmouth, and beat the cowards with his sword at Kip's Bay.
He never could understand how a man could be a coward,
and it was the one thing with which he had no patience.

And treachery, as I have said, was another. He never
could understand how a man who had sworn to be true to
the cause he had joined, could do or say anything that
should be disloyal to that cause. That is why he was so
broken by Arnold's treason and why he was so stern with
André and determined that he should die.

So when this letter from the soldiers came to him, asking

THE GENERAL LOSES HIS TEMPER.
(Washington refuses a crown.)

him to be king, he was very angry. Even to think of such a thing was treachery to the cause of liberty; to say it, was open treason. He had pledged his life for the freedom of America, and now to be asked to himself be the tyrant he had overthrown, and rule as king, made him very angry. " Be assured, sir," he wrote in reply, " no occurrence in the course of the war has given me more painful sensations than your information of there being such ideas existing in the army as you have expressed, and which I must view with abhorrence and reprimand with severity. . . . I am at a loss to conceive what part of my conduct could have given encouragement to an address which to me seems big with the greatest mischief that can befall any country. . . . Let me conjure you, if you have any regard for your country, concern for yourself or posterity, or respect for me, to banish these thoughts from your mind, and never communicate, as from yourself or any one else, a sentiment of the like nature."

To me, boys and girls, this is one of the noblest moments in the life of George Washington. People who have written all about him do not seem to give it much attention; but, when I read the history of the world, and see how many great men have fallen into temptation at just such moments as this that Washington faced, when I see how they were unable to put aside the dream of power, the chance of glory, the opportunity to wear the crown and be king of the land in which they lived, I believe that no mightier, nobler, or grander man ever lived than George Washington. For he, who had the power to say yes, was strong enough to say no; he was true enough and noble enough to be angry that anything of the sort should have been said to him. You may be sure no one ever again suggested to Washington the idea of being king of America.

And when, a little later, the soldiers still called loudly for their pay, and threatened to march against Congress and force it to pay what was due, Washington saw that here was a real danger, and quieted it as no other man could. Instead of scolding, as he might, or of heading his discontented soldiers, he asked them to meet him; and then he read to them

"HE CHANGED THEIR PASSION INTO PATIENCE."

a speech that calmed them, and changed their passion into patience.

At last the day came for the breaking up of the army. The war was over, the British had gone, the trouble between the army and Congress, thanks to Washington's exertions, had been fixed up, and now the general must say good bye to the brave men who had fought by his side, and been his faithful officers through all the years of war.

It was in New York City, and in a famous hotel called Fraunces' Tavern, that he bade them good bye, giving to one a kiss, to another an embrace, and to all, the warm hand-

WASHINGTON'S FAREWELL TO HIS OFFICERS.

shake that told of love and loyalty and tender feeling. Not a word was spoken. Then, still silent and sorrowful, his soldiers conducted him to the water-side. Washington stepped into the boat to be rowed across to the New Jersey shore; he waved his hat in farewell to his companions of so many fields, and the general they so loved left them forever.

Then he went to Annapolis where Congress was in session. Before the assembled body which represented the newly-made United States of America he stood, while all men looked upon him in reverence and respect, and in a short address resigned his commission as Commander-in-Chief of the American army.

Then he went to his dearly loved home at Mount Vernon. He was a simple, private citizen now. He reached home on Christmas eve, and you may be sure that he had, next day at Mount Vernon, truly a Merry Christmas.

CHAPTER IX.

HOW WASHINGTON WISHED TO BE A FARMER AND COULDN'T.

WASHINGTON was like a boy just going into vacation time when he got back to Mount Vernon. A great load had been lifted from his shoulders. For seven years he had borne a strain that few men could have stood so long, and that few could have stood at all. Now the burden was removed and he could think of his farm and his servants and his home matters, without feeling that he must sit down to plan a battle, or wrestle with Congress, or consult with his generals over some important scheme.

For a while he would wake up each morning, almost with a feeling of surprise that he had no grave or important business to attend to that day and that, as he expressed it, he was "no longer a public man, nor had anything to do with public transactions."

When he first returned to Mount Vernon at Christmas time he was almost "snowed under," so severe was the winter. But as the roads became clear, visitors flocked to Mount Vernon to see and talk with the man who had rode away from it one fine morning as just Colonel Washington, and had returned to it seven years later General George

Washington, one of the most famous of the world's great men.

For, try as hard as he might, he could not help being what he said he was not — "a public man." He was the best-known American. He was the one whose advice was most widely sought and most generally followed. Letters came to him from all over the world and were about all sorts of things, from an invitation to visit the king and queen of France, and a plan for civilizing the Indians, to a request to sit for his portrait and permission to call a child after his name. To all these letters, to the management of his large plantation and to the development of his western lands, Washington tried to give his attention; so, what with these things and receiving his visitors, he did not have much spare time.

Mingled with these was his interest in even greater matters. George Washington had gone to the wars a Virginian; he had come home an American. Do you realize what that meant? It meant that he loved his own State, but that he loved his country still more. He was almost the first American to have this broader understanding of things and to foresee the wonderful future of the new nation. But, to be a nation, he knew that two things were necessary for these United States — union and protection. The first could never come about if the thirteen states kept on being selfish, thinking only of their own interests, "pulling and hauling" in different directions; the second could

only be secured by a system of forts and military organiza-
tion in charge of Congress, and by a watchful care over the
Western border-land.

You must remember that when the Revolution closed,

BUILDING A PALISADED TOWN ON THE WESTERN BORDER.

two foreign powers claimed possession of vast sections of
what is now the United States. These were England and
Spain. Washington knew that these two great nations
could keep the United States from making the most of its

Western country and could control the navigation of the
Mississippi River, unless the States were united in protect-
ing and enlarging the western border.   So, before he had
been many days at home, " farming " at Mount Vernon, he
began writing to prominent men in different sections of the
country telling them how he felt about these things and
what he thought the States should do.   " But they cannot do
anything that will last," he said, " unless they agree to live
together under some plan of union, by which they can all
join hands to pull together for the good of all, and to
appoint certain men who should represent them in the coun-
cils of the new nation and some one man to be its head and
its guiding hand."

Even before Washington left the army, at the close of
the war, he had seen what was needed and had written to
the governors of the different States a strong letter begging
them to do something toward establishing a union of all the
States under a central government and, what he called, " a
federal head."   He said the same thing to his soldiers when
he bade them farewell, and so it was known pretty generally
throughout the land what Washington's ideas were, and
people had a way of saying : If General Washington thinks
it is best, then it is best ! "

So, when, from his home at Mount Vernon, where he
had thought all he had to do was to attend to his own
affairs and " run his farm," he began to write letters to leading men, trying to get them to do something, it was seen

that his way was wise and that his advice should be taken. One by one the different States agreed to meet and talk things over. So, after trying to do this at Annapolis in Maryland in 1786, and failing, they met at last at Philadelphia in May, 1787, in what is known as the Federal Convention. There, they went to work to get up some sort of an

"IF GIN'RAL WASHINGTON SAYS IT IS BEST, IT IS BEST!"

agreement by which the thirteen States, and the new ones that might be made later, could live in peaceful union and work together for the prosperity and welfare of the new nation whose freedom had been obtained after so much struggle and privation and danger and death.

It was quite natural that Washington should be the leading man in this Convention. The "coming together" — for that was what "convention" meant — was largely his idea and when he came to it as delegate from Virginia he was elected to be its presiding officer.

Of course you are not to imagine that there were no other great men in America. It would be very wrong for me to so write this story of our great man as to lead you to think that he was the only one. It was the time of great men. There were Benjamin Franklin of Pennsylvania, who

A GROUP OF GREAT AMERICANS.

(1. *Thomas Jefferson.*   2. *Alexander Hamilton.*   3. *John Adams.*   4. *George Washington.*
5. *Benjamin Franklin.*   6. *Samuel Adams.*)

was as wise as he was great, and John Adams and his cousin Samuel, from Massachusetts, great men, both, and foremost in putting the new nation of the United States on the right track; there were Alexander Hamilton of New York, Washington's right-hand man for so many years, and Thomas Jefferson of Virginia, Hamilton's great rival, and, later on, President of the United States; and there were others whose hearts were warm for liberty through the struggle with England and whose brains were busy in trying to think out and plan out just the right future for the nation they had helped to make. These all were great men; but George Washington was the greatest.

The American people believed in him; they felt that he was honest, pure, and strong and that whatever he wished to do or whatever he tried to bring about would be best for the country and for them.

So, when he was made president of the convention that was to arrange for some sort of a compact by which the United States could be joined together and under which they could live, everyone felt that it was the right thing to do, and waited for the result.

You know what the result was —- the Constitution of the United States. You know, because you study it at school, how it commences: "We, the People of the United States, in order to form a more perfect Union, establish Justice, insure domestic Tranquility, provide for the common defence, promote the general Welfare, and secure the Blessings

of Liberty to ourselves and our Posterity, do ordain and
establish this Constitution for the United States of America."

The "people of the United States" did not all of them
like the constitution that their convention agreed upon; it
was a long time before all the States decided to accept it,
but they did, finally, and there is no doubt that George
Washington's name signed to the document — the first of
all the names signed to it — did much to bring people to
believe in it as the best paper that could be made saying
just how the United States should be governed.

It is said that when Washington took his pen to
sign the Constitution he said, thoughtfully and solemnly:
"Should the States reject this excellent Constitution, the
probability is that an opportunity will never again be offered
to cancel another in peace; the next will be drawn in blood"
— all of which means that Washington felt that this was a
most important moment in the history of the United States;
that the Constitution he was about to sign was the very
best thing that the very best men of America could agree upon;
he was certain that, should the people of the several States
say they did not like it and would not have it, no one could
agree upon anything; then quarreling and strife would
follow; all that the Americans had fought for in the revolution would be lost and the people, unable to govern themselves, would fall to fighting to see who should govern,
until, perhaps, in the end, they would be worse off than when
they revolted from King George of England.

"WASHINGTON'S THE ONLY MAN TO BE PRESIDENT"

But none of these dreadful things was to happen, because the people had faith in the men they had sent to the Convention to think and act for them; especially did they have faith in the man who sat in the highest seat as president of that Convention and whose bold and handsome signature, which every boy and girl now knows and honors, was signed to the new Constitution, as much as to say: " I believe that this Constitution is the best we can make as things now stand, and I sign it, not only as president of the Convention that has drawn it, but as one of the people of these United States of America which it seeks to unite in peace and brotherhood."

INKSTAND FROM WHICH WASHINGTON SIGNED THE CONSTITUTION.

So it was, at last, accepted and adopted by all the people of the thirteen States. And, with a few changes, called amendments, so it has continued; and it stands to-day the bond of union between all the States of this great country and one of the most remarkable papers ever written through all the years of the world's long history.

The first section of the second article read: "The executive power shall be vested in a President of the United States of America. He shall hold office during the term of four years, and, together with the Vice-President, chosen for the same term, be elected as follows" — and then it goes on to say just how he shall be chosen.

Well, when it came to the point of choosing the man
who must stand at the head of the new government as its
manager, or " executive," there was but one opinion among
the people. You know, of course, what this was : — that
George Washington, of Virginia, was the one man in
America who ought to be and must be and should be the
president of the United States. This was what everyone
said, thus his friends wrote him and the man who drafted
the most of the new Constitution and who has been called its
"father " (I mean Alexander Hamilton) told him that this
would have to be and that it was his duty to " comply with
the general call " of his country.

As I have told you before, George Washington never
" shirked." Whatever he felt to be his duty he set about
doing, no matter how hard or how unpleasant it might be.
And it is also true that whatever office was tendered him he
accepted, because he thought it was his duty to do so, even
while he did not feel himself smart enough for the place.
This was true about almost every position he accepted, from
the days when, as a boy, he went off with rifle, rod and chain
to survey Lord Fairfax's wild lands among the Virginia
mountains.

So when people told him he was the only man to be
president, he was not at all anxious to have things so turn
out as to put him into the presidential chair, nor was he
pleased at the prospect. He was fifty-seven years old, just
the age when a man feels like settling down and taking

things comfortably, especially if his life had been as busy and as active as Washington's had been. " Let those who wish such things as office or leadership be at the head of things," he said ; " I do not wish them. All I desire now is to settle down at Mount Vernon and live and die an honest man on my own farm."

But this quiet life was not to be his. Much as he wished to spend the rest of his days as a plain Virginia farmer, the people whom he had led to freedom and citizenship decided otherwise. When, therefore, according to the Constitution, the sixty-nine votes of the electors for president were opened and counted, it was found that every one of them — sixty-nine in all — named as choice of the people for president of the United States of America, George Washington of Virginia, and the farming at Mount Vernon had to be given up once more.

CHAPTER X.

THE FIRST AMERICAN PRESIDENT.

I SUPPOSE there is not a boy or a girl who has any sort of " spunk " or ambition but enjoys being at the head of things. It may cost hard work to get there, and may need hard work to hold the place, but, all the same, the boy or girl who is at the head is proud of it, and tries to stay there.

It is so with men and women, too, and the real test of a man's ability, courage and good sense comes when the high position he has attained demands certain duties of him which he must try to do as well as he knows how.

George Washington, as we have seen, would have preferred the easier life of a Virginia farmer; but, even though he said to his friends : " I don't wish to be President; I don't want the office; I shall be sorry if I am elected and have to give up my home for public life again "— still there is no doubt he felt pleased to think that he was so highly honored; and, although he accepted the office of President, as he himself said, " with more diffidence and reluctance than ever I experienced before in my life," he accepted the office with the determination to do his duty, no matter how hard might be the work he had undertaken.   He knew that he had the people at his back.   He knew that they believed in him, and so, leaving Mount Vernon, he rode on toward New York City, then the capital of the new nation.

Every mile of the way must have made Washington feel more ready to enter upon his high position.   For all along the route, bells rang, drums beat, soldiers and citizens turned out, and boys and girls met him with songs and flowers and smiles and ringing cheers.   And yet, though this reception made the American hero gratified and glad, it made him also sad and sober; for he saw, better than any one else, what it all meant — what the people expected of him and how much he must do to meet their expectations and desires.

WASHINGTON'S INAUGURATION JOURNEY. — THE ARRIVAL AT NEW YORK.

It was no easy task he had undertaken, but he accepted it with an earnest determination; and, on the thirtieth of August, 1789, he stood upon the balcony of Federal Hall in New York (where the sub-treasury building now stands, in Wall Street), and took the oath of office.

He was dressed in a dark-brown suit, made of American cloth, with knee-breeches, white silk stockings and silver shoe-buckles. He wore a sword at his side, and his hair was powdered and drawn back into a queue, as people wore it then. He was a noble-looking man, and how proud of him must have been the crowd of people that packed the street, looking on.

He bent above the open Bible and kissed it solemnly as he took the oath of office; the chancellor, or judge, who pronounced the words that Washington subscribed to, stepped forward, and lifting his hand cried out in a loud voice : " Long live George Washington, President of the United States ! " Then a flag shot up to the cupola of the hall and swung out upon the breeze; cannons boomed; bells rang; the people cheered and cheered and cheered ; and George Washington, the farmer's boy, the surveyor, the backwoodsman, the soldier, the statesman, the hero, was inaugurated as the first American President.

All this sounds very grand, but compared with the United States to-day, it was really a very small country and a very few people, that hailed George Washington as president. There were not quite four millions of people in the United States when Washington was inaugurated; to-day there are nearly seventy millions. The settled portion of the country lay along the Atlantic coast, and little or nothing was known of the vast western country from which so many great states have since been made. There were but few cities, and not one of them had more than twenty thousand inhabitants. To-day, Chicago, the site of which was not even known in Washington's day, has a population of considerable over a million, and in the city of New York and the section round about there, live to-day more people than,

FEDERAL HALL IN WALL STREET.
(Where Washington was inaugurated.)

in Washington's day, lived in the whole United States. There were no railroads, nor steamboats; there was neither electricity nor gas, nor matches, nor even oil lamps, for lighting; there were no water works; there were but few bridges, and on the farms there were none of the things that to-day help the farmer, such as mowing-machines, and reapers, and threshers, and stump-pullers and steel ploughs. There were only a few newspapers and these were small and uninteresting; there were but few books, and the schools

THE INAUGURATION OF PRESIDENT GEORGE WASHINGTON.

were poor enough. So, taking it all together, you will see that the boys and girls of to-day would find themselves anything but happy if they should be suddenly set down in the America of Washington's day, with all the wants and none of the comforts of to-day, and told to make men and women of themselves.

But it was these men and women, these boys and girls that Washington was elected to govern and make a nation of. He set about it at once. The first thing he did was to select the men with whom he could talk and work as his advisers. They were to be the heads of the different departments of the government — the State Department, which looked after the things that were to be carried on between the United States and other nations; the Treasury Department, which looked after the money matters of the country; the War Department, which looked after the soldiers and sailors; and the Law Department, which settled questions in dispute, and advised the other departments what to do in such cases. Since Washington's time other departments have been added — the Navy Department, the Post-office Department, the Department of the Interior and the Department of Agriculture; but when the first American president went into office, there were but four of these departments, and the heads or secretaries of these four departments were selected by Washington, and made by him his advisers or Cabinet, as it is now called.

You must not think that because the people hailed Washington as a hero and cheered him as president, that everybody agreed upon the way things were done or ought to be done. They did not. There was discussion, and wrangling, and dispute and quarrelling in Congress and out, just as there is now, and just as there has always been, ever since men began to act for themselves, and tried to govern themselves. This is what makes what we call political parties; and, as there were Tories and Patriots in the Revolution, and as there are Republicans and Democrats to-day, so, when the government was first formed, there were two parties, the Federalists and the Anti-Federalists — those who liked the United States (or Federal) government, and believed in the Constitution, and those who liked best the old plan of the states governing themselves and did not believe in the Constitution. Washington and Franklin were the greatest Federalists, and their following was large.

But Washington knew that even those who did not believe as he did might be men of wisdom, with a right to their opinions. He did not think, as do so many boys and girls and a great many grown folks also, that the person who does not believe as they do is a stupid or dangerous know-nothing. So, when he made up his advisers or Cabinet, President Washington invited, among others, Hamilton, the most earnest of Federalists, and Jefferson, the warmest of Anti-Federalists. He did this because he considered them the best men he could select for the departments he wished to give into their charge; and Thomas Jefferson was appointed Secretary of State, and Alexander Hamilton, Secretary of the Treasury — the two most important places in the Cabinet.

It is often the little things that bother people the most. Now it seems a small thing to worry over, just how to speak of the president, and just how he should see the people. But it turned out to be quite an important affair. You see the nation was new; it was made up of people who had been used to kings and royal governors — both those who respected them and those who disliked them. It is a hard thing to satisfy everybody. Certain of the people thought that, as the head of a nation, the President should have some grand title like His Grace, or His High Mightiness or, as the Senate really decided, His Highness the President of the United States and Protector of their Liberties; others wished to have no title whatever, for fear the presidents should think themselves too grand and "give themselves airs." Washington, himself, cared little for titles. "A grand name is of no value," he said, "if the man who bears it is not worthy or noble, or one who tries to so live and act that the title shall really be suited to him." "It is best to be a plain and simple 'Mr.' if one is but a gentleman," he said. He was therefore really pleased when it was decided to address him just as the Constitution called him — "the President of the United States" and "Mr. President," and the title has remained unchanged from Washington's day to this.

So many people wished to see him from curiosity, on

business or for their own selfish advantage that the President had scarcely time to give to his regular business and to his letters.   In fact, all these calls kept him from attending

to the work he had to do. So he arranged for certain reception days. On Tuesdays, from three to four, he saw all those who wished to call upon him, and on every Friday afternoon the President and Mrs. Washington had a reception, to which the people were all invited. When this was decided upon there were plenty of people to criticise and to say that Washington and his wife were "stuck up," and were trying to be as grand as the kings and queens of Europe; and indeed, as you will soon see, as parties grew and men took one side or the other on

IN WASHINGTON'S DAY.

the questions that were all the time coming up for discussion, there were many who did not hesitate to say things against Washington which some of them lived long enough to be sorry for and to wish they had never said. So, at last, the government was started, with a Congress and a President; and the world looked on and sneered and criticised, or applauded and praised, according as those who sneered disliked and those who praised believed in a people trying to govern themselves without kings or queens, or princes and nobles. For you see, a republic, such as the United States had declared themselves, was an experiment in the world and people did not know how the experiment would turn out. It was well for the experiment and well for the United States of America that the first American President was so great, so noble, so dignified, so simple, so just, so able, so sensible and so good a man as was George Washington of Virginia. It was his wisdom and caution and will that gave the Republic so fair a start and set it so well forward on the road that nothing could stop its progress or do it lasting harm in all the hundred years of prosperity and pride and danger and disturbance that were to follow the inauguration of its first and noblest President.

"THE WORLD SNEERED OR APPLAUDED, CRITICISED OR PRAISED."

CHAPTER XI.

HOW WASHINGTON SERVED AS PRESIDENT THE SECOND TIME.

THE Constitution says that the term of office of the President of the United States shall be four years. But when Washington's first term of four years, which extended from 1789 to 1793, was finished, the people were not willing to give him up. Even those who did not agree with him felt that it was not wise, at that time, to make a change and all agreed that no man in the land was better fitted to be its chief magistrate than George Washington.

So he was again elected to the presidency without a vote against him; and, though he wished greatly to give up the office and go back to his beloved farm at Mount Vernon, he felt that the people wished him to stay where he was and that, for a time at any rate, it was his duty to remain. And thus, on the fourth of March, 1793, he entered upon the office of President of the United States for the second time.

Great things were happening in the world, and Washington's justice, good sense and patriotism were to be tried during his second term as President as they had never before

GEORGE WASHINGTON.

("The Athenaeum Head." Painted from life in 1796, by Gilbert Stuart, and presented to the
Boston Athenaeum. Now in the Boston Museum of Fine Arts.)

been tried in all his long and busy life. The success of the
Americans in their struggle against tyranny, and the forma-
tion of the American Republic had set folks in Europe to
thinking. Especially was this the case in France, where
the king had been the ruling power for hundreds of years
and the nobles had made slaves of the people. Gradually
the people began to talk and then to act, until at last, in
1789, came that uprising of the people, so like and yet so
unlike our own. This was the French Revolution. The
people of France got their tyrants by the throat; they became mad with success, and did many terrible things.
They murdered their king and queen, the princes and
nobles; the men and women who had been in power ran
away or, not being able to get off, staid behind and were put
to death. Alone and unaided France fought all Europe —
fought, defeated and, by the aid of a young soldier who was
not a Frenchman but a Corsican, named Napoleon Bonaparte, finally conquered it — and then lost all it had gained,
because Bonaparte was not a Washington and thought more
of himself than he did of the country that had made him
Emperor.

France, as you know, had assisted America in her struggle
for independence; she had helped to make the United
States a republic. So, when France tried to do the same
thing, she naturally supposed that America would help her,
and there were thousands of people in America who supposed and said the same thing. Especially, when, in 1793,

war was declared against England, and a Frenchman named
Genet was sent to America to fit out vessels, called priva-
teers, to destroy English vessels and ruin the commerce of
England, from which its strength and prosperity came, did
the French republicans think they could do about as they
pleased in the land which, so they said, would not have been
free had it not been for the French help.

Washington saw the danger.   He was full of friendship
to France for the help she had given America, though none
knew better than did he that France gave that help, not
because she loved and pitied America, but because she hated
England.   "But," he said, "if we let France come over here to
fit out vessels and enlist men to fight England, we ourselves
shall soon get into a war with England and that would be
the worst thing that could happen to us now.   America is
weak and poor as yet ; what she needs is peace, not war.
If I let myself be guided by these people who wish to help
France, I shall get the whole country into a bad fix.   It is
best for America not to meddle in the troubles and struggles
between European nations ; she has her hands full in trying
to get on here.   Therefore the United States, in this war
between France and England, must be neutral — that is, we
must help neither the one nor the other.   If we do, it may
be our ruin."

So he preserved what is called "a strict neutrality."
Genet, the Frenchman, who had come across for help,
threatened and blustered and scolded and said all sorts of

MARTHA WASHINGTON

(Painted from life in 1796, by Gilbert Stuart, and owned by the Boston Athenæum. Now in the Boston Museum of Fine Arts.)

harsh and mean things against Washington, and, strange as it may appear, so did hundreds of Americans who should have known better and should have had faith enough in Washington to know that what he did was right. But they did not, and, instead, they made his life miserable by insisting upon his doing things he ought not and would not do. They called him hard names and made ugly pictures of him and did and said many things that we, to-day, knowing how great and good a man he was, cannot understand.

And, with the French trouble came others that needed all Washington's wisdom and firmness and courage to face and settle. The Indians in the Ohio country, which, years before, Washington had struggled over with France for possession, begun to annoy and attack the settlers who were forcing their way into the new lands to make homes and build towns therein. They would not agree to the terms or offers that President Washington made them, but kept on burning and killing until soldiers were sent to punish them. Twice, the soldiers returned unsuccessful, and then Washington collected a large army and sent it out under command of General St. Clair, an old Revolutionary fighter, to conquer the Ohio Indians. He gave General St. Clair all the good advice that so successful an Indian fighter as Washington had been in his young days could give, and especially he said to him, remembering Braddock's terrible defeat, " Beware of a surprise." But St. Clair *was* surprised and, in a defeat almost as bad as was that of Braddock's, his army was so whipped that nearly one half of his soldiers were killed or taken prisoners.

Washington felt dreadfully. Had his directions been followed the war would have been brought to an end. But now he had to do it all over again. This time he sent a brave soldier who had fought well and successfully in the Revolution, General Anthony Wayne. He could not be surprised and he soon whipped the Indians, made them sue for peace and got from them, forever, the present great State of Ohio.

GENERAL ARTHUR ST. CLAIR.

Then there were troubles about taxes among the settlers of Western Pennsylvania, which led to what is known as the " Whiskey Rebellion ; " there were worrying disputes with England as to forts and bounderies in the western country and the stealing of American sailors by English sea-captains ; these were only settled by sending an American to England to try to, make things right, but as this settlement, known as Jay's Treaty (from Judge Jay who was sent to England about the matter), gave up some things to England, many of the people who had not yet got over their hatred for the " mother country," as England was called,

THE POST OFFICE IN WASHINGTON'S DAY.

(*Delivering the mail in the Ohio Country.*)

grumbled and talked about it and found fault with the President. There were troubles in the Cabinet because the members did not all believe alike and were continually disputing or seeking to get the better of one another.

Through all these troubles, Washington moved straight on, doing his duty, saying little, but acting at just the right moment, and so bringing the young nation safely through its years of babyhood and making it ready for a vigorous youth and a sturdy manhood.

But all the worries and anxieties of the time told on Washington's strong nature and made him determined, when his time was up, not to serve again as President.

Election time came around once more, but, though implored to act a third time as President of the United States, and though assured that those who were against him were but a few, a very few, as compared with the whole people, and though it was told him that to put in another man as President while the revolution in France and the wars in Europe were going on would be bad for America, Washington declared that he could not and would not serve again ; he said he believed that the people were united and that a new President, if a wise choice were made, would be able to carry on the government satisfactorily and well. And then, on the seventeenth of September, 1796, he issued his remarkable Farewell Address to the American People.

I wish you boys and girls who read this story of George Washington would turn to your histories and read this wonderful letter to the people of the United States; or, if it is too long, read a part of it. The Address was meant for the people of that day, to be sure, but it seems to have been written, just as surely, for you and for me.

It was, of course, his announcement to the people that he would not serve again as President. But it was more than this; it was his good-bye to public life after forty-five years of noble service; it was a solemn appeal to his countrymen to be true to the country they themselves had freed and the nation they themselves had made; it was a word in warning, a word in advice and a word in love. It implored them to be patriotic, to be united, to be brothers, to be Americans!

And yet, though the loving and helpful words of this noble man were written to his countrymen in affection, in faith, in hope, and in the desire to strengthen and benefit them, the Farewell Address was laughed at and criticised and pulled to pieces and called all sorts of names by some of those very Americans who needed, more than all others, to read and heed it. To-day their memories are unhonored, their words are lost, their names are forgotten; and, though they may have been honest men and really meant all the mean and spiteful things they said, it is for us to remember that the life of a really good man can be made unhappy by those who should think before they speak, but do not; and that the tongue of the slanderer is sometimes as sharp and hurtful as the dagger of the assassin. But, more than all

MOUNT VERNON AS IT LOOKS TO-DAY.

can we feel glad to think that neither slander nor wickedness nor meanness have been able to take away one jot from the name and fame of George Washington.

CHAPTER XII.

HOW THE GENERAL GOT HIS DISCHARGE.

AMID tears and cheers and the warm good-byes of friends and followers, George Washington laid aside the cares of office and went back to his farm in Virginia — that Mount Vernon farm toward which his thoughts and desires had so often turned through the eight years of his busy and anxious life as president.

He found plenty to do. Mount Vernon, in his absence, had been taken care of by an overseer, but things had been allowed to run down, or, at least, not kept up to Washington's idea of what was right; so the first thing he did was to repair and improve things. "I find myself in the situation, nearly, of a new beginner," he wrote to one of his friends. "I am surrounded by joiners, masons and painters; and such is my anxiety to get out of their hands, that I have scarcely a room to put a friend into or to sit in myself, without the music of hammers or the smell of paint."

So he mended and repaired and built and extended, or looked after his broad plantations, glad to get back to the

WASHINGTON, THE FARMER.

free, busy, out-of-door life he had always loved. His door was ever open to the friends and strangers who were constantly coming to Mount Vernon to see the greatest man in America.

For he *was* the greatest man in America. Of that there can be no doubt. Notwithstanding the enemies he had made because of his saying to France: "Hands off! America is not your servant;" and notwithstanding the strong and different ways of thinking about

matters of government that were dividing the people into
what we call political parties; and notwithstanding the harsh
and unfriendly things that leading men and leading newspapers had said about the president, the great mass of people
were of his following and on his side. They could not for-

MOUNT VERNON IN 1800.

get that this strong and silent man had for forty-five years
been at the front in all the great events that had made the
United States possible; they knew his sincerity, his honesty,
his faith in freedom and in the people, his clear vision, his
strong grasp, his wisdom in planning and doing, his modesty,
his ability as a leader, his safety as a guide. For the success

ful soldier they cried: "Hurrah! he is a hero;" for the able president they flung their queer, three-cornered hats in the air and shouted: "Hail to the chief!" for the big, noble-looking, strong and stalwart six-footer, with the calm and handsome face, the well-knit figure and the kindly, courteous but awe-inspiring manner they felt both reverence and affection, and, even as they cheered and shouted and swung their hats, they would say: "See, there is Washington! the greatest man in the world."

GEORGE WASHINGTON.

(*Carved in wood by William Rush: thought to be the most life-like representation of Washington. Now in Independence Hall, Philadelphia.*)

So, even though he was worn out in the people's service, though he was "getting on in years," as the saying is, and longed only for rest and quiet, the people could not do without him, and when the time came and they called him to the front again, he came, as reluctant as ever, but just as ready if the need existed.

The need did exist and the call came speedily. The trouble with France grew grave. The men who overthrew the king, and started the French republic, were not as calm, as cautious or as wise as those who started the American republic. They had no Washington to lead them on. So, as they gained power by killing their king and queen and leading men and women, they grew bloodier and more tyrannical, they became selfish and "cheeky" and, especially toward America, they were arrogant and insulting. They treated the United States as if America owed France a debt, for which payment was always to be asked. "France helped you in your struggle; now you must help France in hers. Give us ships and men; let us use your seaports to fit out our vessels in; or, if not, pay us so much money and we will let you off."

Washington had not liked such talk, and had said so. When he saw how cruelly France had treated her king, and had at last cut off his head; when he saw how she had persecuted and almost killed Lafayette and Rochambeau and other brave Frenchmen who had fought for American liberty; when he saw how unjust and brutal and arrogant and overbearing were the men in power, he said : "We must not yield to France. If we do, it will be bad for us in every way."

John Adams, who followed Washington as President of the United States, said the same thing. And when the French leaders demanded from the American representative money to keep the peace, Pinckney, the American minister indignantly refused, and was driven out of France. Then all America was angry and prepared to fight. "Millions for defence, but not one cent for tribute," was the cry on American lips. It looked like a war with France, and word was sent to Washington at Mount Vernon to leave his farm once more and raise and lead the army of the United States.

Much against his will, but feeling, as he always did, that if the republic were in danger he must do whatever seemed to be his duty, Washington left the quiet of Mount Vernon and hurried to Philadelphia, which was then the capital of the nation. He was appointed lieutenant-general and commander-in-chief of the armies of the United States.

Here again, boys and girls, you may see the greatness of Washington. The greatest is not he who commands, but he who, while able to command, is willing to be commanded. Washington had held the highest office in the gift of the people for whose freedom he had fought. Now, when duty called, he was ready to accept a position below the highest. Other men in his position have, when such an opportunity offered, seized the power and used it to their own advantage. He acted always in the spirit of the Master whom he served and tried to follow — the Divine Leader who said : "Whosoever will be great among you shall be your minister, and whosoever of you will be the chiefest shall be servant of all ; even as the Son of Man came not to be ministered unto, but to minister and to give His life a ransom for many "

At Philadelphia, Washington was soon deep in work again, organizing and appointing officers in the new army that was being recruited for the French war that all men thought would surely come. But Washington was getting to be an old man — too old, at least, for the wear and tear of

DRILLING RECRUITS FOR THE WAR WITH FRANCE.

life in the saddle and the field as a soldier, and, in accepting command of the armies of his country, he had only asked one privilege: that he should not be compelled to serve in the camp or the field until it was really necessary for him to do so.

After he had got everything ready, and had appointed

his chief helpers, and seen to the comfort of the soldiers and the new recruits — he was always great for doing that, you know — he went back to Mount Vernon, to attend to his plantation, and put things in order in case he should be called away again. For, whatever happened, Washington was always ready.

He was ready now; and all too soon the call came. But it was a call that few men expected, though all men knew it must some day come. It was the call to the soldier, the statesman, the patriot, to come up higher. The call came as suddenly, as unexpectedly, as sharply, as ever on the battlefield his orders to his soldiers had been issued; and he met and obeyed it as calmly, as uncomplainingly and as willingly as he had taught his followers to obey.

Washington was now nearly sixty-eight; he seemed to be as well, as strong and as vigorous as ever; he had scarcely ever been ill; there was not the least sign that sickness could lay him low, and he rode and walked and looked after things on his farm and conducted the affairs of the army as wisely and as well as ever.

But one cloudy day in December, 1799 — the twelfth of the month — just after he had finished a letter urging the establishment of the school for soldiers, now known as the Military Academy at West Point, he mounted his horse and rode away to visit different points of his big farm where work was being done. A snow storm caught him, while he was riding: it turned to hail and then to rain and the Gen-

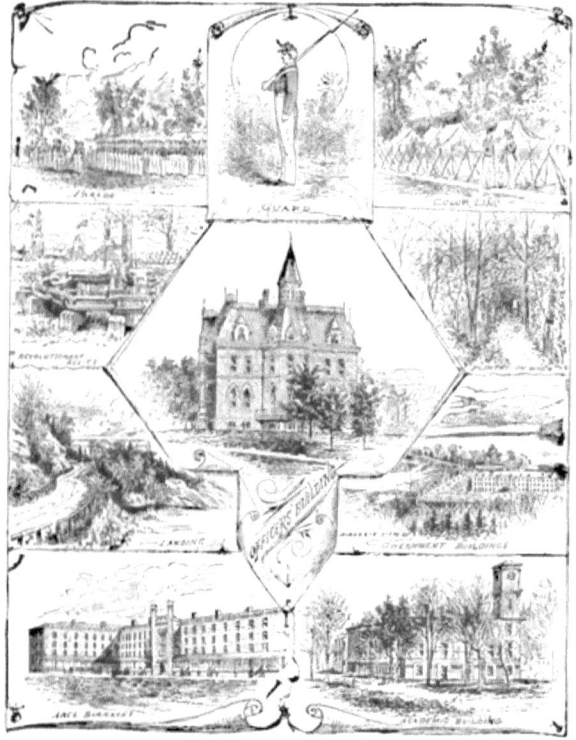

ONE OF WASHINGTON'S RECOMMENDATIONS.
(The U. S. Military Academy at West Point, N. Y.)

eral came home wet and chilled. The next day he had a
sore throat, but rode out to see about cutting down some trees
and then went home again. His cold increased; he had a
chill and then a difficulty in breathing. The doctors who
were called could not help him and he grew worse. He had
what was then called a "quinsy sore throat"—a sort of
croup or laryngitis, as it is called to-day.

He called his household around him ; he said he knew he was going, but that he was "not afraid to go ;" he thanked the doctors for their efforts, gave directions to his beloved wife and his faithful secretary, and with the words " it is well " upon his lips, answered the call that had come to him. With his fingers upon his own pulse, calmly counting the feebly-coming strokes, at eleven o'clock on Saturday night, the fourteenth of December, 1799, George Washington the American bade good-bye to the world he had served so well by living in, the land he had helped so much by his loyalty and his love. The old General had his discharge.

When the news went abroad, saying "Washington is dead," friends and foes alike hastened to pay tribute to his memory. The two powers against which he had stood out most sturdily — monarchical England and republican France — hastened to express their sorrow and their respect. In the midst of a great pageant of rejoicing because Napoleon Bonaparte was returning a victor from his battles in Egypt, the standards and flags of the French army, which Americans thought Washington might have to lead them against in battle, were draped in black, and " Bonaparte, First Consul of the Republic " decreed a statue to Washington. At almost the same time the great Channel fleet of England, riding at anchor in Tor Bay on the Devonshire coast, lowered the flags of every frigate and every vessel of the fleet to half-mast, thus honoring a foeman that England had faced in fight, but respected, honored and mourned.

"A REVULSION OF SYMPATHY AND SORROW."

And his own land which he had so loved and labored for, sorrowed deeply for its loss. Congress adjourned at once, the Speaker's chair was draped in black, the Congressmen put on mourning; there were resolutions passed, and speeches made, and memorial services held all over the land; and wherever, in cities or villages, on fishing-boat and workbench, in the farmhouse, the schoolhouse, and the homes of the wealthy and the poor, the sorrowful tidings came, there was mourning and sorrow, there were words of praise, of reverence and love, for the general called from his army, the planter from his farm, the husband from his home, the foremost citizen from the land he had served so nobly — Washington, "first in war, first in peace and first in the hearts of his countrymen."

THE TRIBUTE OF THE NATIONS.

CHAPTER XIII.

WASHINGTON'S BOYS AND GIRLS.

SOMEHOW or other, we are always interested in hearing about the home-life of famous folks — where they live and how they live, how many children they have, and even what they have for breakfast and how they spend their time.

This is perfectly natural; for, when we know people, we like to know them well; and when we have become interested in a great man's story we are glad to become acquainted with the surroundings amid which that story told itself. So we like to know how Longfellow lived at Craigie House and where Dickens loved to walk about Gads Hill. We are interested in reading about Lincoln's love for his boy Tad, and how Shakspere used to play with his little granddaughter, Lizzie, and how anxious Columbus was that his son Diego should be rich and powerful.

It is not always safe to gratify this desire, for sometimes the men of whom we have made heroes, do not bear close inspection, and the men who are great in the world often prove to be very small at home. But when we come close to George Washington, we need have no fear of being ashamed of our hero.

MRS. ALEXANDER HAMILTON,
of New York.

MRS. RUFUS KING,
of Massachusetts.

MRS. JOHN JAY,
of New York.

MRS. WILLIAM BINGHAM,
of Pennsylvania.

MRS. ROBERT MORRIS,
of Pennsylvania.

MRS. THEODORE SEDGWICK,
of Massachusetts.

MRS. JAMES MONROE,
of Virginia.

MRS. JAMES MADISON,
of Virginia.

MRS. CHARLES CARROLL,
of Maryland.

SOME OF THE LADIES OF WASHINGTON'S "PRESIDENTIAL CIRCLE," 1789–1797.

When we hear that he had no children of his own we feel, at first, that it was a pity that he had no one to follow him and bear his name in direct descent to the future. But we can console ourselves with two thoughts: sometimes, great men's children do not always turn out a credit to their fathers — indeed, one writer has recorded, with satisfaction, that George Washington had no son to disgrace the name

THE COLLEGE OF WILLIAM AND MARY, WILLIAMSBURG, VIRGINIA.
(*Where was Washington his commission as surveyor, and of which he was Chancellor*)

he had made so great and glorious; the second thought is the one that a great American long ago put into beautiful words: "Heaven left him childless that his country might call him father;" and the "Father of his Country" George Washington has been called to this day.

But that home-life of Washington which we all like to

know about, and of which I have now and then given you a
glimpse, was really one of the best and most beautiful things
about this great man. We know how dearly he loved his
fine home at Mount Vernon, and how, when he was most
successful, as well as when he was most bothered and per-
plexed, his thoughts would turn to his big and fertile farm
on the banks of the broad Potomac, and how the desire " to
live and die a private citizen on my own farm," was expressed both in his talk and in his letters.

To that "farm," after the wedding festivities were over,
he took his wife, the fair young widow Custis, and here, with
their mother, came Washington's step-children, John — the
six-year-old boy whom they called " Jacky " — and the little
four-year-old girl Martha, known to the homestead as
" Patty."

It was a fine home for Jacky and Patty Custis. Mount
Vernon, as many of you know, is a beautiful place to-day; in
Washington's time it was a splendid Virginia plantation,
with broad acres of rolling farm-land, and a lawn sloping
down to the sparkling Potomac, with fruit and flowers in
abundance and a house that afforded plenty of play room
for children.

Colonel Washington, the children's step-father, was then
a tall and noble-looking gentleman of twenty-seven ; their
mother, whom all the world now reveres as " Martha Washington," was a "small and stately lady," who looked after
her son and daughter very closely, as was the way with

JOHN PARKE CUSTIS AND MARTHA PARKE CUSTIS—"JACKY" AND "PATTY."
(*From an original painting.*)

parents in those days. The little boy and girl studied their lessons and did their tasks dutifully and well. Matilda, or Patty, was, we are told, a demure little lady who wore her hair "done up" and adorned with "pompons," and was brought up by her mother to work on "samplers" and study housekeeping, and be diligent and quiet and "correct." Jacky, being a boy, had a little more freedom; but he, too, had to study hard; his step-father, who as we know was one of the best surveyors in America, taught him engineering and military tactics and instilled into the boy that deep love of out-of-door life that was a part of his own nature.

Washington was always inclined to be more "easy" with his step-children than was their mother; and, before his real duty of "nation-making" called him from his home, he was with them much at Mount Vernon, and tried to act toward them as if they were his own son and daughter. Very often he and Jacky went "a-hunting," and very often, too, they "catched a fox" together, as Washington notes in his diary.

Both Jacky and Patty were delicate children. Indeed, the pretty little girl did not live to grow up, but died in 1773, when she was but scarcely seventeen. A letter, yellow with age, is still in existence in which her step-father tells of his grief and sorrow over the loss of "the sweet, innocent girl — dear Patty Custis." Jacky, however, outgrew his delicate boyhood and lived to have children of his own. He became his step-father's "aid-de-camp;" and he saddened for George Washington the glorious close of the Revolution ; for he sickened and died at Yorktown just after the surrender of Cornwallis. And when he died, Washington, who had watched over him so carefully and loved him so dearly, threw himself, as we are told, at full length on a couch and wept like a child over the sad and sudden taking off of his " dear Jacky."

When Colonel " Jacky " Custis died he left a widow and four children. And Mount Vernon was so lonely without the young life and gayety that Washington loved, that he begged for two of the children to bring up as his own. Mrs. Custis finally consented, and Washington adopted a girl and a boy — Eleanor Parke Custis, two and a half years old, and George Washington Parke Custis aged six months.

These children were brought up at beautiful

ELEANOR PARKE CUSTIS ("NELLIE").

Mount Vernon, as their father and his sister had been before them ; and, even to-day, " Nellie Custis " — the bright, charm-

ing, wilful and loving girl of Mount Vernon — is an ever-
present memory as the visitor walks through the rooms of
that historic house. She was "the general's" pet and pride,
his companion in ride and walk, his ardent admirer as he
was hers, and the one who, by witty or saucy remark, could
set a-laughing the man who, his critics declared, was never

NELLIE CUSTIS'S ROOM AT MOUNT VERNON.

known to laugh. Her room at Mount Vernon is still
shown to visitors, her "harpsichord," or old-fashioned piano,
for which the general paid a thousand dollars and presented
to her, is there too, and about the old mansion linger many
traditions of the good times "Miss Nellie" and her brother
"Tut" had when they were the children of Mount Vernon
in the days after the Revolution. It swarmed with visitors
then, and was full of life and gayety   Its stables and its

dog-kennels, its garden and its "preserves" were filled with animals and with the rare and beautiful things that came as gifts to Washington from his admirers all over the world.

"Tut," as Nellie's brother, George Washington Parke Custis was nicknamed, was a bright little fellow — "a clever

NELLIE'S PIANO OR "HARPSICORD."
(Now at Mount Vernon.)

boy" his grandmother, Mrs. Washington, called him — and "the general" in his leisure hours looked carefully after his bringing up. He was educated at Princeton College and at Annapolis, and General Washington, then President, wrote the boy many letters of advice, suggestion and help. That they did him good, we know; for he grew to be a man of gentle manners and fine tastes, the author of "The Life and Letters of Washington" and the owner of the beautiful mansion now known as Arlington, on the Potomac, just across from Washington City. It was the home of his son-in-law, Robert E. Lee, and is now the National Burying Ground of a host of the soldiers who fell in the Civil War. Both Nellie and Washington Custis lived to be old people; and, when Washington Custis died in 1857, in him passed away the last male representative of the family of George Washington.

So many years of Washington's life were public ones, passed in the service of the people as leader of their armies or as the head of the nation, that the home-life he loved so much was largely denied him. But, whenever possible, he had the children with him. They made a "triumphal progress" to his inauguration, and during his term as President they were frequently with him. And when Nellie became the wife of Lawrence Lewis, the general's private secretary, she made Mount Vernon her home, and was there with her new little baby the sad night that Washington died.

GEORGE WASHINGTON PARKE CUSTIS.
(*From an ivory miniature.*)

There were other boys and girls, not of the immediate Mount Vernon household, who were always welcomed there and who were dear to Washington and his wife. If any preference existed — and with "the general" it must be confessed that such a preference did exist — it was in favor of girls. Mr. Moncure Conway tells us how he loved to have the little Custis girls with him and adds, "it was so through life. In the most critical week of his presidency, that in

which the British treaty was decided — the second week of
August, 1795 — Washington went to the house of Randolph,
Secretary of State, and played with his little daughters."

He would walk up and down the great portico at Mount
Vernon with a little toddling girl holding his finger — that
great finger that the baby hand could scarcely encircle, and
many a dollar went for toys and keepsakes for the children
and grandchildren of the various Custis' households. Some
of those very keepsakes are now preserved as heirlooms by
the descendants of the little folks to whom they were given
so many years ago.

As Washington grew older and more famous, young peo-

THE PORTICO AT MOUNT VERNON.
(*Where Washington played with the children.*)

ple had that awe of him
that boys and girls are
apt to feel for great men,
and were not easy in
his presence. This made
Washington feel badly, for
he liked a good time; he
liked to dance and play
games, and he did not like

to feel that his presence put a damper on sport. There is
a story told that, at a young people's party, when the fun was
"fast and furious," President Washington came into the
room; at once the fun stopped, and every boy and girl
were on their good behavior. Like dear old Colonel New-
come in Thackeray's story, Washington saw that his pres-

THE WASHINGTON FAMILY AT MOUNT VERNON.

(Copied by George P. Fernald from an old painting.)

ence was a bar to the frolic, and after a few pleasant words
he left the room, whereupon the young folks' dignity turned
into fun again. But Washington had felt badly to think
that he could not be in a good time; so, when the frolic was
again at its height, he slipped quietly up to the open door-

PRESIDENT WASHINGTON.

way and, unseen by the boys and girls, watched the sport and
enjoyed it immensely. All of which shows that greatness
has its drawbacks, and that fame is sometimes a fun-spoiler.

But the same love of sport that made Washington the
boy a leader among his comrades, lived with him all through

life; and, when he was among his girls and boys, even his
dignity would relax and he would join with them in their
good times. We read of his having had "a pretty little

WASHINGTON AND THE "LITTLE COCKADE MAKER."

frisk" with a houseful of young people. Indeed, "Nellie"
Custis said of him that, though "a silent, thoughtful man,
the general would unbend when there were children in the
company;" and, she added, "I have sometimes made him

laugh most heartily from sympathy with my joyous and extravagant sports."

So you see that our hero had about him much of the real man after all, and was not the "marble statue" that so many would have us think him. He loved children, and the boys and girls loved him. There are many stories told of his interest in boys and girls and his tender ways toward them ; such, for instance, as the story that Miss Seward tells of Simon Crosby, "the little cockade maker," who rode his shaggy pony to Washington's camp with a load of cockades and epaulets — all he could contribute toward the cause — and implored "the general" to accept them. Lafayette and Hamilton, scarcely more than "big boys," were his closest friends in the army, and the British, in derision, called the brave young French noble "the Boy." Jacky Custis and Lawrence Lewis, both boys, were very near and dear to him ; and, so strong was his belief that upon the boys and girls of his day depended the future success or failure of the nation he had helped to found, that, in his will, he left money for four different educational enterprises ; while, in his famous Farewell Address, he wrote for the benefit of young Americans, quite as much as for their fathers and mothers, the words of advice and direction that his countrymen have ever remembered and, sometimes, tried to live up to.

CHAPTER XIV.

THE STORY WITHOUT AN END.

THE GREAT WHITE DOME.

NOW that I have told you the story of George Washington's life, does it seem to you a very remarkable one? If you are looking for something exciting, or for something full of adventure and surprises, you may, of course, be disappointed; for George Washington was simply a Virginia gentleman who did his duty and helped his fellowmen.

He was not perfect; he had his faults, as do all of us. He could get very angry when things went wrong, and could say and do things that made men afraid to face him. He was not the precious little prig that certain unfounded stories of his boyhood make him appear, who could cut down his father's pet cherry-tree, and then strike an attitude and say, as if he were speaking a piece: " Father, I cannot tell a lie, I did it with my little hatchet." But he never told a lie, and through all his long life he hated nothing worse than falsehood. In the heat of passion, as when Lee traitorously ordered a retreat at Monmouth; when he detected men making money out of the woes and worries of the Revolution; or when St. Clair, in the face of his repeated charge to beware of a surprise in fighting the Ohio Indians, fell into the trap, and was desperately defeated, this quiet, calm and cool man could swear and rage; but he detested an oath, and one of the first things he did upon taking command of the army at Cambridge was to issue an order requesting his soldiers not to swear. He has been known to cuff and strike his soldiers when they were cowardly, quarrelsome and stupid; but no commander of armies ever looked more carefully after the men under his lead,

THE TOMB OF WASHINGTON AT MOUNT VERNON.

was more beloved by them or was followed more willingly.

I suppose we could find faults and flaws in everyone's character, if we set out to hunt for them; but that is not what we are sent into the world to do. We want to find out the good points of men and women, of boys and girls, and if the faults that we see or read of are so many or so big that we cannot help seeing them, then we are to use these very faults as warnings for our conduct, to escape them, or steer clear of them if we wish to be good men and women — even if we may not be great ones.

Now, what made Washington great? We admit that he had faults; but who remembers them now, or tries to pick them out? If you recall the life of Columbus, the Admiral, which opened this series of Children's Lives of Great Men, you will recollect that he had very great and detestable faults, and was capable of doing things that really good men like Washington and Lincoln would not have done for all the wealth of the Indies, nor all the gold of Carthay. And yet Columbus is to-day one of the world's great men; his faults are forgotten; only what he achieved is remembered.

Of Washington, we set down this: as a boy he was honest, upright, truthful, obedient and brave — liking out-of-door life and out-of-door sports, and entering into everything so heartily that he soon became the leader of his playmates, and the one that all other boys who knew him looked up to ("tied to," as the saying is), and followed; as a young man, he was reliable, adventurous, courageous, manly, pure and strong — doing whatever task was set for him as well as he could, never grumbling, and never shirking; as a man, he was what we call a leader of men — clear-headed, clean-hearted, seeing what ought to be done and doing it, or setting others to do it when he had shown the way, never trying to get the best of others, never jealous, never disturbed

GENERAL GEORGE WASHINGTON OF THE AMERICAN ARMY.
(*From the painting by John Faed, called " Washington at Trenton."*)

by the jealousies of smaller men, however hard they tried to upset his plans or injure his reputation, a planner of great things, and a doer of them as well, just the man for just the work that the making of a nation demanded.

He was not born great. He grew into greatness. He was not a bright nor a brilliant boy; but if he had anything to do he set about doing it at once. And as he grew older and mixed with men, he saw that what made men respected and obeyed by others was reliability -- that is, keeping one's promises, and promising only what one felt he could do.

There are some

WASHINGTON'S HANDWRITING AS A MAN.

people who object to what is called "hero-worship;" but if a man is worthy to be called a hero, then it is well and wise for men and women, especially for boys and girls, to set him high in their hearts, to look up to him, and to call him great and grand and noble. Only, boys and girls, be careful how you pick out your hero. Not the conqueror, who, like Napoleon Bonaparte, though a mighty genius, was, still, simply brave and smart and selfish, who loved war and power simply for his own ends, and because they brought him what he desired — not such a man is worthy to be selected by you as a real hero; not the man who is powerful because he is rich, or because he is strong, or because he is smart, alone, is to be chosen by you as your hero; but the man who, knowing what is right, dares to do it, and, doing it, is able to do it nobly and well, the man whose work is not for himself, but for the good of others, who is courageous, strong and honest, loving, tender and true, who can command and counsel, but is himself willing to obey and to take advice, who is a leader of men, but a lover of men also, who is noble because he is good, and great because he is noble — that is the man you can take for your hero, and thank God that such a man really has lived and labored and succeeded in the world. And such a man was George Washington.

The people who, as I have told you, object to hero-worship are ready to criticise Washington. They will tell you that he was not an American, but only an Englishman who happened to live in America when America was really English; they will tell you he was cold and stern, and unloving; that he was great, as a mountain or an iceberg is great, but not such a man as boys and girls would love if they knew him, or would care to hang about or cling to, if they were with him; they will tell you that he never laughed, that he never played, that he never joked or did any of the things that make men pleasant comrades and good fellows.

To all of which things you can answer: "It is not so." No man was more an American than Washington. He, first of all, saw the great future that was in store for the people he had made free, and the nation he had founded. He was cold only to those who tried to use him for selfish ends; stern only to those who proved themselves unworthy, cowardly, traitorous or disloyal; unloving to no one, not even his enemies. The man who, when a young Indian fighter, was so moved by the woes of the people on the frontier as to say : " I solemnly declare I could offer myself a willing victim to the butchering enemy, provided this would contribute to the people's ease;" who could love his mother, even like a little child, when he was both general and president ; who, as

A PEN PORTRAIT OF PRESIDENT WASHINGTON.

we have seen, was a favorite with children and especially to little girls; who could make such young men as Hamilton and Lafayette cling to him in affection and admiration, and could kiss his officers good-bye when the war was over, and the day of parting came — this was surely not a cold, a stern nor an unloving man.

The man who has the care of a nation on his shoulders, who is naturally grave, silent and sober, does not go about

poking fun at people, "cutting up," or being what is called
a "hail fellow;" and yet we know that Washington enjoyed
a good time, a hearty laugh and a pleasant company.

But these things, after all,
are not for us to consider.   As
the years pass, the greatness
of Washington grows on the
world.   His story is not yet at
an end; and it will never end,
while men and women honor
nobility of character, while boys
and girls love to hear the story
of how a farmer's boy grew
into a hero, and a simple gentleman into a great man.   His
story will never end, for the
world will never cease to love,
to honor and to reverence the
name of George Washington.

And how his country has
honored him!   It holds him as,
above all others, its mightiest
man.   The capital of the nation
bears his name, and is built, a
beautiful city, upon the spot

THE WASHINGTON MONUMENT.
(*In the City of Washington.*)

he selected, while, above its splendid streets and its magnifi-
cent buildings and its glorious white dome, towers the mighty

WASHINGTON CITY — THE CAPITOL AND PENNSYLVANIA AVENUE FROM THE WHITE HOUSE.

shaft that has been reared as his monument and memorial.
The home he loved so dearly at Mount Vernon is the most
sacred spot in all the land, sought by pilgrims from all over
the world, as one, in foreign lands, visits the shrines of saintly
men. On the far Pacific coast a great and growing state
bears his name, and, all over the land, towns and counties,
streets and parks, schools and institutions and banks and all
the things that people most prize and most work for, honor
the memory of Washington by bearing his name.

And how grandly has the country
which he helped to form and which he
led to victory and a future, made his
predictions come true! Its four millions
of people who hailed him as president
have grown to nearly seventy millions,
its thirteen states to forty-five, its four
cities to more than four hundred, any one

THE SEAL OF THE STATE OF
WASHINGTON

of which is more populous than the most populous city of
Washington's day. The American leads the world in enterprise, energy, invention, prosperity and patriotism; and, under
the folds of the banner of the stars and stripes, schools and
churches flourish as in no other land, homes are happier, men
and women freer, boys and girls better, and the future more
certain and more secure than in any other land upon the
whole round earth.

And all this is because George Washington lived a hundred years ago; and that is why his story, as I have assured

you, was not yet come to an end. It never will end, while the world stands, and fathers and mothers teach their boys and girls to reverence worth and greatness, truth and honor, nobility and goodness, strength and purpose, grandeur and success — all of which are chapters in the ever-living story of George Washington, the noblest American.

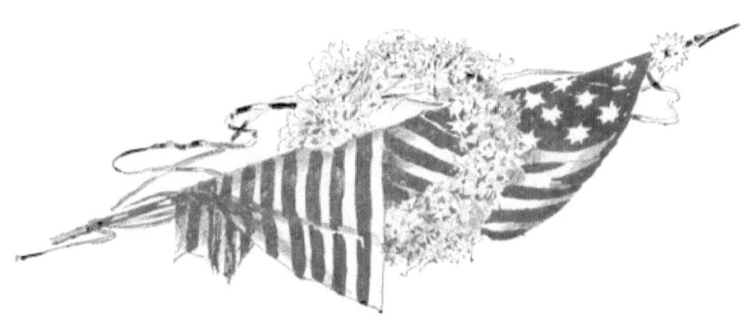